## Horror Show

Lyons went for the eyes first, striking with the Tiger's Claw, digging for the soft membrane and raking with his nails. Then pushing off from a sunken log, he brought his knee up into the groin and began to tear at the throat. He heard a groan, felt a wash of bubbles as the hands around his neck began to yield. Finally, twisting with another pounding jab, he broke for the surface.

Air.

Lyons heard the eerie moan, saw the eyes roll back to reveal the bloody whites. He had the advantage and linking an arm around his opponent's throat, Lyons simply began to squeeze.

"Able Team will go anywhere, do anything, in order to complete their mission."
— *West Coast Review of Books*

**Mack Bolan's**

# ABLE TEAM®

# ABLE TEAM.
## Cult War

### Dick Stivers

A GOLD EAGLE BOOK FROM
# WORLDWIDE.

TORONTO • NEW YORK • LONDON • PARIS
AMSTERDAM • STOCKHOLM • HAMBURG
ATHENS • MILAN • TOKYO • SYDNEY

First edition June 1990

ISBN 0-373-61248-6

Special thanks and acknowledgment to
Ken Rose for his contribution to this work.

Printed in U.S.A.

**1**

*Nothing is coincidental in New Orleans.*

It was Friday, eight o'clock in the evening, still warm. With its cap of gray clouds, the city might have been encased in a bell jar. There were occasional cracks of dry thunder to the west, but not even the hint of a breeze. For a long time after returning to his bedroom and frantically searching for his fifty-dollar pair of tennis shoes, Inspector Antoine Dunn clung to the railing and gazed out across the gardens of tangled vines, monstrous camellias, fig trees, willows and moss-encrusted oaks. Then, by degrees, he shifted his gaze to the end of the path, where someone had left a chicken claw dangling from the iron gate.

*Nothing is coincidental in New Orleans.*

Dunn was a tall man with a triangular face and a narrow mouth. Although there were those who detected a trace of Cajun in his eyes, he was actually pure Irish—a second-generation cop, a third-generation boy from New Orleans. Still, there was nothing in his heritage to prepare him for what was happening now.

As far as Dunn could remember, it had all started last Monday—another gray and windless Monday with sterile thunder from the west and an oppressive sense of damp stagnation. Having received a whispered telephone call at seven o'clock in the evening, he had found himself in Storyville with a twenty-two-year-old informant who called himself Ray Shay. A wiry mulatto who vaguely resembled a rabbit, Shay had never been held in particularly high regard by members of the New Orleans Police Department. But since the man claimed to have information concerning the unusually nasty murder of a dealer named Charlie Craw, Dunn felt obliged to listen.

They met in a crumbling warehouse below the Point. As always, Shay was dressed in Levi's, T-shirt and raincoat, all black. Also typical of the man, he refused to say a word until Dunn laid down the money: first twenty, then twenty more, then still another twenty.

"This better be good," Dunn said. "For sixty bucks this better be real good."

Shay merely smiled, then slipped a hand into his raincoat pocket and withdrew a genuinely disgusting claw.

"What the fuck?" Dunn demanded. "What's that? A goddamn chicken foot?"

"No, man, this here ain't just a chicken foot. This here's *gris-gris*. You understand what I'm saying? This is genuine *gris-gris*."

"*Gris-gris?* What the hell's *gris-gris?*"

"*Gris-gris* is what makes it work, man. It's what gives the power to believers and helps them talk to the spirit world."

"What spirits? What are you talking about?"

At that point Shay's lips split in a skeletal grin. Then he whispered, "Voodoo, man. I'm talking *voodoo*."

After pondering Shay's revelation, Dunn finally asked, "Okay, so what the hell is this all about?"

Shay slid him a slow and easy smile. "It's about what's happening around here. It's what gives them the power."

"I'm tired of playing twenty questions with you, Shay. What power?"

Nervously the informer looked over his shoulder. "The power to call down the spirits, man. The power that be in *macumba*."

They receded a little deeper into the warehouse and away from the long shafts of moonlight. In addition to the chicken claw, Shay had also brought what looked like a cat's skull and the dried ear of a pig.

"Dig it," Shay said. "You dudes have been trying to find out what happened to Charlie Craw, right? You boys figure someone maybe whacked him real good, because maybe he was stepping on some toes, right? Well, that ain't exactly what happened to Charlie Craw. What happened to Charlie Craw was that he got whacked by *macumba*. He got cursed and he got hexed, and then he got his heart cut out by some freak with powerful *macumba*."

"And this freak with the powerful *macumba*, does he have a name?"

"He's got lots of names, man. He's got more names than the Devil himself."

"Fine, but what do people call him to his face?"

Then, although Dunn eventually had to lay down another forty dollars of Department money, he finally got a name: Duval. Baby Shu Duval.

At the outset the lead had actually seemed quite promising. According to State Narcotics, Charlie Craw did have a rival named Baby Shu Duval. The man was described as a thirty-five-year-old Haitian male, black, two hundred and twenty pounds. Although the DEA had no specific record of Baby Duval, there were definite indications that he was involved in the sale of at least cocaine and marijuana, and possibly the transportation of Mexican Brown. Then, too, there were indications that his operation was expanding north along Canal Street into Storyville, a move that would have certainly put him in conflict with resident dealers like Charlie Craw.

But, if all that seemed to make perfect sense on one level, on a somewhat darker and less obvious level, something was very wrong. To begin with, people were scared, genuinely scared. "Hey, you don't talk about Baby Duval around here," a Burgundy Street bagman had told Dunn. "You hear what I'm saying? You don't even *talk* about him." While four blocks closer to Storyville, people were hesitant to even pronounce the man's name.

Next, after repeated queries to Washington, Dunn began to realize that Baby Shu Duval was a special case in more ways than one. Not only did Immigration have no record of the man, but the FBI wouldn't even acknowledge his existence.

And finally there were the voices.

As far as Dunn could figure, the voices had begun on Wednesday—a bleak and rainy evening wrapped in river mist. Having received word that Baby Duval might have initially entered the city with a four-time loser named Jackie Griff, Dunn took another easy drive into Storyville. There he found a half-stoned Griff nodding in a cold-water flat above a cannery. Like most of the junkies along the Strip, Griff was a starving hustler with one foot in the grave. Supposedly once a lightweight contender, he had fled to New Orleans after beating a man senseless in a Port-au-Prince bar. Nineteen months on the crack express, however, had left him unable to make a fist.

"This is how we're going to play it," Dunn said after kicking down the door and slamming Griff against the wall. "It's called stick and carrot. You don't answer my questions, I'll feed you to the catfish. Cooperate, and you'll walk away with a brand-new twenty-dollar bill. Now, do I have to explain the rules again?"

"No," Griff breathed through a mouthful of blood. "I understand."

But the moment Dunn mentioned Baby Duval, Griff suddenly grew stupid again. To begin with, he claimed he'd never known Duval, never even heard of him. Then, following another brief meeting with the plaster, he admitted he knew the man but couldn't seem to remember much more. At that point Dunn lost his temper and withdrew his persuader—a four-inch sand-filled blackjack.

"Tell you what we're going to do," he told the junkie. "We're going to start playing baseball. We're going to pretend we're in the majors. So, unless you start telling me about Baby Duval, I'm going to hit a homer with your fucking head.''

But Griff just shook his head. ''Ain't nothin' you can do to me, mon, dat would be worse den what Baby does. Because Baby got da power. You dig it, mon? Baby got da power.''

''What kind of power?''

''Da black power, mon. Da black power of *quimbanda*.''

''Yeah? So what's *quimbanda*?''

''*Quimbanda* is da worst kind of voodoo power. *Quimbanda* is da kind of voodoo power dat gets you in da night. It's da kind of voodoo dat drive you crazy and den leaves you weak so dat dey can come and cut out your heart.''

''You mean like what they did to Charlie Craw?''

''Dats right, mon. Like what dey did to Charlie Craw, and maybe even like what dey do to you if you don't be careful.''

''What are you raving about?''

''I mean, if you keep askin' questions about Baby Duval, den maybe Baby gets mad. You know what I mean, mon? Maybe he gets mad and send some zombies to cut out your heart.''

''Zombies?''

''You know, zombies, mon. Guys dat be dead but still be walkin' around and doin' the biddin' of da Voodoo Prince. Guys dat you can't shoot and can't stab because dey already be dead. So, if you keep askin' questions about Baby Duval, maybe da zombies get you, too. Maybe dey come in da night and cut out your heart.''

Dunn just laughed in Griff's face. But later he started hearing the voices.

It was about nine o'clock when Dunn left Storyville, about half past ten when he left the Camellia Bar and Grill on St. Charles Street and nearly eleven when he finally returned to his apartment. An hour later he finally crawled into bed. The wind, whistling through rainspouts, sounded like a thousand sighing souls. The thunder, echoing out of the east, sounded like cannon fire. But in the end there was no mistaking the voices...softly calling to him from deep inside the walls: *"Gris-gris. Gris-gris. Gris-gris. Quimbanda."*

The following morning he found a slaughtered cat dangling from the branches of the fig tree outside his window. Two days later he discovered a pool of blood on his doorstep. And now there was a chicken claw dangling from the iron gate.

*"Gris-gris. Gris-gris. Quimbanda."*

Dunn lighted a cigarette and sagged against the window box. There had to be a logical explanation. He ran a hand across his forehead. Maybe he had a fever, or the beginning of another headache. He shifted his gaze to the far wall where something seemed to be crawling across the plaster. A spider? A moth? A scorpion?

He reached for the telephone, thumbed through his Rolodex, then finally decided that no one would believe him, anyway. Taking another long drag on his cigarette, he let his head fall back against the cool plaster. Although the walls were silent now, he knew it wouldn't be long before the voices started again. *"Gris-gris. Gris-gris. Gris-gris. Quimbanda."*

He shifted his gaze back to the dangling chicken claw, then back again to the spidery shadow on the molding. There was also a green chameleon perched on the window ledge, but he doubted there was a connection. After all, New Orleans gardens had always been filled with chameleons, and the fact that one was now perched on the ledge was probably just a coincidence—except, of course, that if Dunn had learned anything during the past five days, it was that there were no coincidences in New Orleans. There were signs, and there were omens, but there was no such thing as a coincidence.

Then, suddenly, he heard footsteps on the floorboards in the hallway outside. A minute later the doorknob turned slowly and he was on his feet immediately, reaching for his snub-nosed .38.

Unfortunately Dunn had forgotten that you couldn't kill a zombie.

He emptied his revolver into the chest of the hulking black man who crashed through the door—six clean rounds that hardly even slowed the monster. Then, grabbing the neck of a bourbon bottle and swinging it like a club, he smashed the human freight train on the side of the head, a blow that should have dropped the bastard to his knees. But Dunn might as well have hit him with a flyswatter.

The New Orleans cop struck again with the jagged bottle as the monster closed in, a hard jab to the belly that tore through a ragged T-shirt but didn't seem to penetrate the flesh. Then he lashed out with a snap kick to the groin, but the man merely smiled at him, the broad lips spreading to reveal a set of black teeth, the bloodshot eyes reduced to slits as a truly enormous black fist seemed to descend from the ceiling with the force of a hammer.

In the next moment Dunn was only conscious of the weight, the enormous weight that pinned his shoulders to the floor. When he finally caught a glimpse of the knife, he tried to twist free of the grip, but by then there were other hands holding him down—dark and incredibly powerful hands that seemed to materialize out of thin air.

He managed another blow before they finally plunged in the knife, but it was only a feeble one. Then, although he must have let loose with one long, piercing scream, he was really only aware of the cold steel tearing into his stomach, slicing up between his rib cage and finally closing in on his still-beating heart.

**2**

"Something tells me you're not going to want to see this, my son."

Inspector Renny Lussac responded with an easy smile, gazing past the coroner to the room's interior. "Don't you worry about me, Paulie. I'll be fine."

Also present were three uniforms, two boys from forensics, the landlady, a neighbor and a second homicide inspector named Osmond Massard. Apart from the coroner, however, none of them had actually looked at the body...or at least not for more than a second or two.

At first glance Antoine Dunn looked like any number of victims Lussac had seen over the seven and a half years he had served on the New Orleans Police Department. Although there were at least three pints of blood on the floor, a multiple stabbing always left a lot of blood. Although the eyes were wide in frozen horror, that, too, wasn't unusual. Indeed, it wasn't until Lussac had actually entered the room, moved past the long shafts of morning light and then fixed his gaze on the mantel that he began to appreciate the coroner's advice: *Something tells me you're not going to want to see this, my son.*

While Lussac stared at Antoine Dunn's heart, which rested on a porcelain dish amid a swarm of bluebottle flies, the coroner smiled and growled, "As I said, it's not a pretty sight."

Lussac tapped out a Camel, stuck it between his lips with automatic grace and shifted his gaze back to the body. A tall, thin man with wavy red hair, lean features and blue eyes, Lussac was one of only three full Cajuns on the force. At twenty-nine years old, he was also the youngest full inspector, and it was rumored that he had the most interesting love life.

"How about you just tell me the facts?" he said at last. "How about you just tell me what they did to him?"

The coroner shrugged, ran a handkerchief across his ample jowls and pointed at a heap of entrails adjacent to Dunn's left arm. "Well, in simple terms, my son, they did exactly what appears to have been done—struck him several times on the face and head and then opened the chest cavity with one hell of a sharp instrument."

"And how many do you suppose there were? I mean, to hold him down and all?"

The coroner shrugged, hitched up his trousers and glanced back at the body again. "Two, maybe three, depending, of course, on just how strong they were."

There were sounds of retching from the corridor, then the unsteady footsteps of Osmond Massard. A slow-moving bear of a man, with more than twenty

years in Homicide, Massard had never really over-
come a propensity to lose his lunch at a crime scene,
in this case, four cups of coffee and an order of eggs
Benedict from the Absolute Bar and Grill.

"Oh, my God," Massard slurred, easing through
the doorway for another long look at the body. "Oh,
my God in heaven."

There were more sounds of retching from the bath-
room, then a soft-spoken forensic technician named
Harper told Lussac that there was something he ought
to see. "Not that I'm pretending to do your job," the
lanky technician added, "but I do think you might
want to take a quick peek at this here revolver."

Lussac picked up the weapon with a pair of sur-
gical tweezers and examined the empty chamber.
"So?" he asked with a quizzical frown.

"So most likely it was fired at the perp—all six
rounds."

"Which leaves us with the question of where are the
holes, or the blood?" Massard asked. "That your
point, son?"

"Exactly," Harper drawled. "I mean, you just
don't shoot six slugs from a .38 without leaving a trace
of something."

"Maybe he discharged the weapon earlier," Lussac
suggested. "Maybe it wasn't even loaded to begin
with."

"Or maybe," the coroner said from the opposite
end of the room, "those bullets embedded themselves
in someone that just don't bleed. I mean, maybe, just
maybe, there's someone or something walking around

right now with six little slugs in his body and he don't even know it. Now what would you boys say to that?''

At that point in the investigation, however, neither Renny Lussac nor Osmond Massard felt confident enough to say anything.

IT WAS FOUR O'CLOCK in the afternoon when the various pieces of the Antoine Dunn murder were assembled in a manila envelope. Among the contents were two black-and-white photographs of the heart, four photographs of the chest cavity and a long view of the body. But what ultimately fascinated Renny Lussac were the nine bloodstained pages of notes concerning Dunn's investigation of Baby Shu Duval.

In order to fully examine the notes and to discuss their broader implications, Lussac and Massard adjourned to the Café du Monde across from the French Market. Although the sky remained gray and the air moist, there was an odd cooling wind from the river, and the air was alive with the scent of camellias wafting from high-walled gardens north of Jackson Square.

"I don't suppose you ever actually witnessed one of them voodoo rites now, did you?" Massard asked between sips of his café au lait. "Sneak out to some old graveyard and watch them folks slice up those poor chickens? Don't suppose you ever did something like that now, did you?"

Lussac smiled and deftly planted another cigarette between his lips. "No, sir, I can't say as I have."

"Well, let me tell you something, boy, it's a sight to behold. I mean, you and I can sit here all day and propose all kinds of fancy theories about what might have happened to poor old Antoine, but until we come to terms with Baby Shu Duval and his spirit world we might as well be spitting into the wind."

Lussac, however, merely smiled again as the smoke slowly drifted from his nostrils. Then, gently tugging on the sleeve of his black linen jacket and shifting his long legs beneath the wrought iron table, he said, "Well, that may be, *cher*, but spirits don't kill people. People kill people."

A waiter arrived with a plate of spiced crawfish and hickory-grilled shrimp in butter and pepper sauce. For the moment, however, Lussac's eyes remained entirely fixed on the women—four, five, a dozen young women drifting like swans along the promenade.

"All right, then," Massard said at last, "how about you tell me what happened, hmm? How about you explain how poor old Antoine fired six slugs from that snub-nosed .38 of his with no effect at all? Not to mention all the other little problems connected with this case."

Lussac tore his gaze away from the women, took another drag on his cigarette and began to pick at a crawfish. "And what little problems are those, Oz?"

Massard shrugged. "Well, for example, I happen to have it on very good authority that Antoine was a little upset toward the end, upset about things that were happening to him."

"Such as?"

"Such as certain strange ailments, certain strange artifacts turning up in his garden and strange sounds heard at night...or at least that's what he was complaining about to the chief the other day."

Lussac shredded the meat from his second grilled crawfish and slowly sucked out the juice. Then, letting the shell dangle from his fingertips, he spread his lips into another easy smile. "Well, all I can say, Oz, is that it don't take much magic to sing in a man's window when the moon is full, or tie a little chicken foot to his doorknob. In fact, it don't take no magic at all. But if you truly feel strongly about all that, then just maybe there's some people I can talk to."

"And just what kind of people would those be, Renny? Friends of your papa?"

"No," Lussac said, smiling. "Friends of my mama."

ALTHOUGH RENNY LUSSAC may have appeared somewhat skeptical about the alleged powers of Baby Duval, in fact, he wasn't skeptical at all. After all, he was the son of Mad Margaret Marsalis.

It was another gray Saturday when Renny Lussac returned to the neighborhood of his youth. Although there was rain in the city, the backwoods were merely fogbound, the moss-draped oaks rising up like humped beasts, while a wind, foul and damp, carried the haunting cries of egrets and the stink of deep-water sloughs.

Although his immediate family had long since moved to Baton Rouge, they still remembered Renny well enough here. They also still recalled his mother, sisters and half-crazed father, who was said to have traded his soul to the Devil in exchange for a chicken gumbo recipe.

It was two o'clock in the afternoon when Lussac reached his destination, an old clapboard house on a lonely suburban road lined with more twisted oaks and ghostly cypress. He was happily received by Miss Charlotte Kacoo, a sixty-year-old black with Choctaw and Caucasian blood, a coppery skin and long wisps of gray hair. Also present was Dame Kacoo's younger brother, a corpulent mulatto whom everyone called Mr. Synn. Then, too, there were the dozens of ancient spirits that Miss Charlotte and her brother were said to have regularly communed with in order to assist the living.

Sweet jasmine tea was served in what Charlotte called her sitting room, a circular chamber overlooking a garden filled with mimosa, spidery ferns and palm fronds. Beyond the garden walls lay a view of the river, where a slow-moving barge drifted on bottle-green water.

It began on a typically easy note with vague recollections about Lussac's family. As Charlotte talked, she continually toyed with a peacock feather and pulled at loose threads on the antimacassar. Mr. Synn, seated in a massive bentwood rocker by the window, hardly even moved his eyes.

"But obviously you didn't come out all this way just to reminisce, child," Miss Charlotte finally said, smiling.

"No, Ma'am, I didn't."

"Then how about you just tell us what's troubling you, *cher*? Maybe Mr. Synn and I will see if we can help."

Lussac took another sip of jasmine tea and turned to the window, where the barge still seemed suspended in time. Then, lighting a cigarette and running an idle finger along the edge of his chair, he said, "Well, it's about this certain bad old boy who calls himself Baby Duval."

Mr. Synn reacted first, pressing a finger to his lips and violently shaking his head. Then it seemed as if Miss Charlotte couldn't quite catch her breath. There were also sounds of a baby crying, but it might have just been the wind.

"Not that I'm suggesting you're acquainted with the gentleman," Lussac added, "but you've heard of him."

"Oh, we've heard of him," Charlotte replied. "My Lord, yes, we've definitely heard of him."

"But he's bad," Mr. Synn growled from the corner. "That's the first thing you've got to know, my son. That there Baby Duval is real, real bad."

Lussac withdrew a battered leather notebook and a pencil stub, then lighted another cigarette. "It's mainly just the background I'm interested in," Lussac said. "It's mainly just what folks have been saying about him, if you know what I mean."

Miss Charlotte sank a little deeper into the chintz and drummed her crimson nails on the varnished mahogany. "Well, now, child, the first thing you must understand is that neither Mr. Synn here nor myself are particularly attuned to the dark side. Now and again we might hear things, yes, but the dark side is by no means our specialty.''

''Because when you start fooling with the dark side,'' Mr. Synn added, ''your only real friend is the Devil.''

There were echoes of a foghorn from the water, followed by what might have been the bark of an alligator. But when Miss Charlotte began speaking again, the silence couldn't have been more complete. ''He's new to these parts,'' she began. ''That there is the second thing you've got to understand, child. Mr. Baby Shu Duval may be powerful as old Nick himself, but he's still pretty new to these parts.''

''And where do they say he comes from?'' Lussac asked.

Miss Charlotte shrugged. ''Well, nobody knows for sure, but my guess be somewhere down south. Somewhere like Port-au-Prince.''

''But that don't account for his power,'' Mr. Synn added. ''The only thing that account for his power is what you might call his liaison with old Mr. Eshu himself.''

''And who's this Mr. Eshu, if you don't mind my asking?''

Charlotte smiled, coyly twisting a gray lock around one dark finger. ''Mr. Eshu, honey, is what the dark side is all about. He's the one who comes in the night, singing songs of Africa. He's the one who whispers in your sleep, '*Gris-gris. Gris-gris. Gris-gris. Quimbanda*'."

"He also be the one who wears that old black cape, that old black hat, that fancy red vest and them nice polished shoes," Synn added. "But sometimes you can only recognize him by his iron trident and the fact that he sounds like a bullfrog."

"Not that Mr. Eshu is purely evil," Charlotte continued, "because no soul is purely evil. But there's no doubt he would lend himself to the practice of evil on account of his greedy nature."

"And this practice of evil would include...?"

"Oh, my child, it would include all sorts of troubling ventures. Making a body ill so he curls up and dies, bringing a body the worst kind of bad luck and maybe even killing off his livestock."

"And what about using those nasty old zombies in order to work his evil deeds?" Lussac asked. "Could a person like Baby Shu Duval really use the spirits to animate a corpse?"

Miss Charlotte smiled. "Well, I do hear tell. I do definitely hear tell."

"Hear tell what, *chère*?" Lussac whispered.

"That Baby Duval derives much of his power from strange substances, and strange substances are what make the zombies walk."

Lussac figured it was time to go. And although Miss Charlotte had difficulty moving, what with arthritis and all, she still insisted on accompanying the young police inspector down the wooden steps and out into the overgrown garden. There were mushrooms here, dark and spotted under the shadows of the cypress trees. And there were monstrous camellias, palm fronds, veils of moss and bluish roses bristling with thorns. But what really caught Lussac's attention, holding his gaze like a magnet, were the motionless chameleons watching from the ivy wall.

"Some folks will tell you they're evil, too," Miss Charlotte purred. "Some folks say all you got to do is stare into their little beady eyes in order to glimpse the Devil's soul. But frankly I never did believe all that, or least ways not about *my* chameleons."

She tore off a wand from a feathery fern and gently extended it to the wall. The chameleon blinked, then shot out its tiny forked tongue.

"No, sir, not *my* chameleons." Miss Charlotte shivered and tossed the fern away. "Although I do declare, child, there's definitely a particular sense of evil in the air, most definitely a particular sense of malignancy in the air around this town."

"And this malignancy," Lussac said softly, "how would you suggest a poor boy like me counter it? I mean, if it was in my mind to stop it, how would you suggest I begin?"

The old woman responded with a sad smile and laid her weathered hand on Lussac's shoulder. "That there happens to be one dangerous question, child. That there happens to be one very, very dangerous question."

"But if I had it in my mind to stop it, Miss Charlotte."

"Then I'd have to say you best go see someone with a little more power than myself, a real live *Babala*, a priest of the cult."

"And where would I find such a person, Miss Charlotte?"

"Oh, they be around, child. If your need is great enough, they be around. But before you go out and start looking, I think there's something else you should know about that ol' Mr. Baby Duval, something that was told to me in the very strictest confidence, but which I will now pass along to you if you promise to use it wisely."

"I do, Miss Charlotte. I certainly do."

"Well, then, child, hear me on this point. According to those in a position to know, your Mr. Baby Duval has himself a little secret, a little dark and nasty secret that he's never told a soul."

"And what's that, Miss Charlotte?"

"Well, I'll tell you. You see, although your ol' Mr. Baby Duval may have come from the southern latitudes, word is that his power is derived from the north. Do you understand what I'm saying, child? Word is that your Mr. Baby Duval derives his power from certain high and mighty white folks in the north."

WHEN LUSSAC RETURNED to the station, he found Massard hunched in front of a computer terminal, pecking at the keyboard with his index fingers and chewing a wad of gum that must have been the size of a baby's fist. From the doorway and in the weak light of the venetian blinds, Massard looked a little like a basset hound with his loose jowls, big ears and sad eyes. While Lussac had been discussing zombies with a half-mad Choctaw witch, Massard had been methodically making inquiries with the various federal agencies: Immigration, FBI, DEA. So, as Lussac moved through the doorway and poured himself a cup of coffee, he asked Massard, "What's the verdict? Is our man a demon or just another Haitian drug dealer?"

"Maybe he's a little bit of both," Massard replied. "Maybe he's one of them strange creatures that crawls like a snake but sucks your blood like a bat. And I'll tell you something else about this here Baby Shu, he may not have cut a deal with the Devil, but he sure as hell cut a deal with somebody."

Lussac emptied a packet of sugar into his coffee, then swung a long leg over the back of a folding chair. "What are you talking about, Oz?"

Massard extended a plump hand across the littered desk and snatched a coil of paper that had spewed out of the fax. "Now I may be just a poor country boy," he said with a lazy drawl, "but I know when someone's trying to pull the wool over my pretty blue eyes." He tossed the fax to Lussac. "Take a look at that, boy, and tell me what you think."

Lussac quickly scanned the terse response from the DEA, the dismissive reply from the FBI and the downright hostile words from Immigration. "So you think someone in Washington's hiding something, that it?" he asked.

Massard shook his head and sighed deeply. "Well, it sure looks strange to me. I mean, here we got ourselves a *known* drug dealer with *known* connections to some mighty impressive distributors, and our brothers in Washington claim they've never even heard of him. And if they had heard of him, they wouldn't tell us nothing, anyway. Now don't that seem strange to you?"

Lussac pursed his lips, then rapped his fingers on the desktop. "How about Interpol? I mean, seeing how we're dealing with a foreign-born suspect, maybe Inter—"

"Also never heard of him, and also resents the inquiry."

"All right, then, how about the National Crime Assistance in Houston?"

Massard shook his head. "And don't ask me about Tobacco and Firearms, because they just told me to go to hell."

Lussac picked up another stack of fax papers. Among them were two more hostile responses from the DEA and what amounted to a cease-and-desist order from the regional FBI director. Also on the desk, though, were three statements from local informers who claimed Baby Duval was involved in major drug operations.

"Well, I guess that leaves us with only one choice," Lussac said at last.

"Yeah, and what's that?"

"Take a walk along that same spooky road that Antoine walked. I think it's time we start ruffling a few feathers, kick a little ass and generally make a nuisance of ourselves until we draw some fire.''

"Yeah? And what do we do if Mr. Baby Duval sends some of his zombies after us?''

Lussac smiled. "Now, you don't really believe in all that, do you?''

IT WAS JUST after nine o'clock in the evening when Renny Lussac returned to his home in the Vieux Carré. Lussac's apartment was a sparse but spacious affair with whitewashed walls and hardwood floors. Below the French windows was a typical New Orleans walled garden of exotic wildness, home to numerous stray cats. But when voices began to echo up from the miniature jungle, there was no confusing them with the cry of restless felines.

In addition to his .38 revolver, Lussac had a .357 Magnum and a Remington automatic shotgun on hand. He also had his daddy's Marlin squirrel gun. But the Marlin wasn't really a weapon; it was a memory. So, when he finally decided to move out into the garden, he chose the Remington, then spent a few minutes listening to the unearthly whisper below, repeating, *"Gris-gris. Gris-gris. Gris-gris. Quimbanda."*

What with the clouds and vandalized streetlamps, the night was very dark. But as Lussac neared the garden gates, the hunched shadow of someone or something slowly swaying beneath a cypress was unmistakable.

*"Gris-gris. Gris-gris. Gris-gris. Quimbanda."*

The flagstones were covered with decades of moss, which effectively muffled Lussac's footsteps. And a hint of a breeze rattling the leaves helped muffle the sound of the first shell sliding into the Remington. But when he finally eased back the gate, the squeal of the rusty hinges was loud enough to wake the dead.

The shadow turned, then hesitated. Although the features were still draped in shadow, the outline of an enormous, muscular black man in a shabby raincoat and tattered jersey was plain enough. So was the knife.

Lussac leveled the shotgun at the man's chest, eased off the safety and smiled. "New Orleans Police," he drawled. "How about you drop that blade and spread 'em?"

In response, the man stepped a little closer.

"You hear me, son?" Lussac asked softly. "You're facing a member of the New Orleans Police Department and I've got a shotgun pointed at your heart. Drop the knife!"

But the man just moved closer, and now Lussac could see the smile. The guy was as big as a barn and jerked forward like a robot. Then, slowly raising the knife he roared and threw himself at the police inspector.

Lussac waited until the man was almost on top of him, then slowly, calmly, just like his daddy had taught him, he squeezed the trigger. The blast caught the man square in the chest, lifted him into the air and tossed him back into a nest of vines, where he lay for at least fifteen seconds before slowly rising to his feet again, another grim smile pasted on his face.

A lot of things passed through Lussac's mind as he watched the monster approach again. He thought about the stories of zombies his mama used to tell, and how the only way to stop one was to pack its mouth with sand. He thought about the legends of bayou creatures that could only be killed with a willow stick. He thought about the stories of prowling phantoms that couldn't be killed at all. But at the same time he also thought about what Miss Charlotte had said about Baby Duval's power coming from the north. And so, as the black killer covered the last few steps, Lussac squeezed off a second shell . . . this time at the head.

The assassin wavered for a moment, a look of stunned surprise in his eyes as the left side of his face literally disintegrated in a cloud of shredded flesh. Just before he hit the ground, he rasped, *"Quim . . . banda,"* then fell silent forever.

Lussac approached the body carefully, the Remington still locked and loaded, his finger still on the trigger. He nudged the lifeless corpse at least three or four times before kneeling beside it. Although the fingers of the man's left hand continued to jerk for at least another minute or two, the right eye was definitely lifeless and the hulk had no pulse.

According to stories from the old people, the source of a zombie's power lay in some sort of magical ointment extracted from the puffer fish and mixed with the blood of a hanged man. It was also said that a zombie's strength was derived from the Devil's breath. But when Lussac finally lifted the killer's tattered jersey, he discovered a far more mundane explanation—a four-ply, high-impact bulletproof vest.

## 3

It was three o'clock in the afternoon when Carl
"Ironman" Lyons, Hermann "Gadgets" Schwarz and
Rosario "Politician" Blancanales, the members of
Able Team, landed in New Orleans. Having arrived at
the airport half an hour earlier, Lussac had grabbed a
bite to eat at one of the concessions. When he spotted
Able Team, he was chomping on a blackened shrimp
and quaffing his second beer.

As Lussac watched the three men approach the bar,
he sized them up. The tallest one, obviously Carl
Lyons, had blond hair and icy blue eyes. Although the
man wore loose-fitting clothes, Lussac could easily tell
that he was quite muscular. Blancanales, on the other
hand, was dark and compact and had the look of a
street fighter. The third member of the Team,
Schwarz, was gray-haired and at least forty-five, but
he, too, looked like someone you didn't want to rile.

"Welcome to the Big Easy," Lussac said when the
commandos reached him. "My name's Inspector
Renny Lussac. I'll be your contact man in the area.
I've taken the liberty of booking you three fourth-

floor rooms at the Holiday Inn, but if you'd prefer something with a little more atmosphere..."

Blancanales smiled, then drawled, "Well, seeing as how this adventure will eventually be billed to the Feds, how about a suite at the Richelieu?"

"And a table with a view at Galatorie's" added Schwarz with a smile.

SEVERAL HOURS LATER Lussac and Massard finally got together with Able Team to talk about their problem. In many ways it was a fitting evening to discuss someone like Baby Duval, what with a warm, damp bayou wind rifling through the city and fog hugging the ground like a blanket of undulating steam. To add to the mood, they could hear the mournful sound of distant foghorns, the faint echo of drums and someone singing from deep within the soot-smeared buildings nearby.

They sat in Lyons's two-room suite, which overlooked a courtyard and old Ursuline Convent. A lazy ceiling fan cast shadows across the rich upholstery, and a low moon seemed trapped in the cypress trees beyond the French doors. Although no one had been particularly hungry, Massard had ordered up a plate of spiced shrimp, crawfish and beer and was busily munching away as they talked.

"The first thing you should understand," Lyons began, "is that we don't exactly represent an official government presence. If things start getting physical, we'll have no problem continuing this operation. But if things suddenly move into a legal arena, we're gone."

"So, then, what exactly *is* your jurisdiction?" Massard asked.

"I guess you could say we kind of work between the jurisdictional lines," Lyons replied. A party of businessmen emerged from the bar below and staggered out into the courtyard, causing Lyons to pause for a moment. "We've actually been watching your Baby Shu Duval for some time," he finally said.

"Since April," Schwarz added. "Since his name started popping up in connection with large shipments of cocaine."

"But it wasn't the drugs that interested us," Lyons continued. "It was Duval's apparent connection with certain federal investigative bodies."

"And exactly what bodies would those be?" Massard asked.

"We're not sure," Blancanales replied with a slow shake of his head.

"But the fact is," Lyons continued, "ever since he arrived from Haiti, Duval appears to have maintained some sort of working relationship with members of a federal agency."

"Working relationship?" Lussac asked.

Again Blancanales shook his head. "We're not exactly sure what the guy's really up to."

"It's mainly the little things," Lyons said.

"What kind of little things?" Massard asked between sips of beer.

"Things like the FBI not following up on leads. Things like the DEA dragging their heels and Immigration losing records. We've also seen some indication that Baby Duval might have had a little deep-cover help establishing himself as one of the premier cocaine lords."

"And by deep-cover help you're talking—" Lussac began to ask softly.

"CIA," Schwarz replied. "We're saying it's possible, just possible, that Baby Duval has a friend in the CIA."

"But why?" Massard drawled. "I mean, what in the world would the CIA want with a guy like Baby Duval?"

"Well, that's why you guys called us in, isn't it?" Lyons replied. "We aim to find out."

Lussac grinned at Lyons. It was time to get down to the nitty-gritty. "The first thing you boys have to understand about our end of this case is that New Orleans isn't just another city. New Orleans is a state of mind. Now I'm not going to try to convince you that there's such a thing as black magic and prowling zombies. But by the same token, you're just going to have to accept the fact that a lot goes on in this town that can't be explained rationally. And regardless of your personal beliefs, you've got to bear in mind that there are a lot of people who *do* believe in black magic and zombies. And that's where Baby gets his power— from the believers."

Lyons took a sip of beer and looked thoughtfully at Lussac. "I thought you said the guy you pasted the other night was wearing a vest."

"I did," Lussac replied, "but that doesn't mean there aren't strange things going on in this city, real strange things."

"Listen, guys," Massard said, "you've got to understand that Renny here is a full-blooded Cajun, and Cajuns tend to view things a little differently than the rest of us."

"But no different than the folks who believe in Baby Duval," Lussac added, rising from the sofa and stepping to the French doors. "It's like one of those lingering nightmares. Even after you crawl out of bed, you can't be certain whether it really happened or not. Now, I'm not saying there's any truth to all that talk about Baby Duval having cut a deal with the Devil, but just the same, there's folks out there that believe it, folks that believe it real hard."

"How many are we talking about?" Lyons asked.

Lussac turned, as if suddenly snapping out of a trance. "How many what?"

"How many people do you figure are behind Duval?"

Lussac shrugged and slowly returned his gaze to the fog-shrouded lanes below. "Impossible to tell," he whispered. "But I can tell you this. That ol' Baby Duval is one sly boy."

"So how would you suggest we proceed?" Blancanales asked, now also gazing down at the deeper shadows where something or someone seemed to be singing the same phrase repeatedly. "I mean, given the fact we know next to nothing about this guy, how would you suggest we proceed?"

"Well, the first thing I'd suggest," Lussac replied, "is that maybe we should take a little stroll on down the streets and see what Mr. Baby Duval has cooked up for you boys now that he knows you're in town."

Schwarz smirked as he picked up a Remington automatic shotgun, not unlike the one Lussac had used three nights before. "What was that you were saying about shooting zombies?"

"I don't recall saying anything about it," Lussac replied, withdrawing a .38 Police Special.

They descended by the utility staircase in order to avoid an awkward confrontation with members of the hotel staff. Lussac took the lead, moving as silently and gracefully as a cat. Lyons was behind him, followed by Blancanales, Schwarz and Massard. When they reached the delivery entrance that led to a narrow lane below the courtyard, Lussac motioned the others into the shadows.

"Now I realize you guys have had a fair amount of experience with this kind of thing before, but I'd like to remind you that New Orleans is like no place you've ever been. Things happen here that have no explanation, things that you might not even see until it's too late. So my advice is to play it slow and easy, if you know what I mean."

Beyond the narrow lane that skirted the courtyard lay a maze of alleys and cartways that had hardly changed in more than a century. The odor of candles, dry rot and pepper drifted on the wind, along with the sounds of whispering conga drums, steel guitars and clattering spoons. A smiling devil had been spray-painted on the ancient bricks of a boarding house, and a bronze plaque, half-eaten by time and pollution, told of a yellow fever plague that had ravaged the neighborhood in the summer of 1832.

Lussac motioned the others into a darkened doorway and pressed himself against the bricks. Although Schwarz and Blancanales had finally fallen silent, smirks of disbelief still festooned their faces.

"So?" Schwarz whispered, rolling his eyes. "Where's da voodoo, huh? Where's dat ol' voodoo magic I been hearin' about?"

Lussac shook his head and exchanged a quick glance with Massard, then slid a little deeper into the shadows. "They're playing with us in the hopes of drawing us onto their ground."

"So maybe we should oblige 'em," Blancanales drawled in a poor imitation of the inspector's accent.

Lussac shook his head again. "Something tells me it's not going to be that easy."

They moved out along an adjoining alley, a particularly foul place with heaps of discarded vegetables, splintered packing crates and newspapers that the rain had pounded into pulp. Except for the distant rhythm of the congas, the neighboring lanes had suddenly grown very quiet. Even the dogs had stopped barking.

"How come I get the feeling we're just chasing shadows?" Blancanales whispered to Schwarz.

"Because that's the way they want you to feel," Lussac replied.

"Yeah, well, then maybe we should wait until they're ready to play for real," Schwarz said, "because this shit is definitely —"

Just then a faint chorus of voices spilled out of the deep pool of fog at the end of the lane.

"I call you at midnight. I call you at dawn. I call you with a bowl of blood and a big cigar, Exu, Exu and pretty Promba-Gira!"

"What the fuck is *that*?" Blancanales growled.

Ignoring the question, Lussac slid along the brick wall until he reached Lyons. Then, snapping off the safety on his revolver, he pointed at the end of the lane and said, "Something tells me they're ready to play hardball."

"So what do you suggest?" Lyons asked.

Lussac glanced up at a narrow flight of stone steps that led to an ancient arcade. "How about I circle around the back while you boys try to draw them out?"

Lyons turned to Massard. "How about it, Oz? You want to lead me and my team down the street a ways while Renny circles behind from the alley?"

Massard shrugged and pulled out his .38 Police Special. "Long as you watch my tail, boy. Long as you watch my tail real good."

"Don't worry," Lyons said. "We'll be right behind you." Then, turning back to Lussac for a last word of good luck, he found the man was gone, vanished into the fog. He couldn't recall having seen anyone vanish so quickly, not in a long, long time.

Voices sounded from the rooftops, and a childlike falsetto chanted from a nearby storm drain.

"Just don't think about it," Lyons told Schwarz and Blancanales as they followed Massard into the mist.

But Blancanales was paying more attention to a shape looming up in front of them. "Jesus," he whispered. "Will you look at that!" Then a second and third figure materialized out of nowhere.

"Well, if these guys think I'm going to buy that old trick," Schwarz breathed, "they've got another think coming." But before he could level his weapon, the figures receded into the mist.

Beyond the end of the lane stood a row of cypress trees and a garden wall plastered with vines. Massard tried to motion the others into the doorway of a hair salon, but Schwarz and Blancanales didn't respond . . . not with another three ghosts emerging from the trees.

"You see what I see?" Schwarz whispered.

Blancanales shrugged. "I'm not sure. What do you see?"

As the figures solidified, their eyes began to glow.

"Just be cool," Lyons said softly. "Be real cool."

But Schwarz had already leveled his shotgun, snapped off the safety and curled his finger around the trigger.

"Don't do it, Gadgets," Lyons said.

But Schwarz had already started to squeeze, not just his finger, but his whole hand. "If you think I'm going to take shit from some voodoo freaks," he rasped, "you got another think coming." By the time he got off his first shot, though, there was nothing to shoot at. He fired off several more rounds, but the only response he got was laughter. And then the voices started up again.

"I call you at midnight. I call you at dawn with a big cigar and a bowl of warm blood, Exu of Intersections."

Schwarz lowered his shotgun, took a deep breath of humid air and glanced uneasily at the rooftops. "You ever see *Night of the Living Dead*?"

Blancanales nodded and smiled grimly. "Yeah, I saw it."

"Seeing as how this is your city," Lyons said to Massard, "I kind of think it's your call."

Massard shook his head. "Like I told you, Renny's the real Cajun. I'm just your regular everyday cop."

"All right," Lyons rasped. "Let's just keep moving."

"Maybe we should have brought some garlic," Blancanales whispered as he continued to move along the damp pavement beside Schwarz and the others. "And some wooden stakes."

"I think you've got your movies confused," Schwarz countered. "Garlic and stakes are for vampires."

"Okay, then how about a clip of silver bullets?"

"Werewolves," Massard said, smiling. "Silver bullets are for werewolves."

"All right, then how the hell do you kill a zombie?" Blancanales shot back.

"You can't," Massard muttered.

They passed a junk shop filled with rusting toasters, transistor radios and old curling irons. There was also a stuffed cat in the window, a mangy, moth-eaten thing with hideous green marbles for eyes. When Schwarz caught a glimpse of the cat, he turned and leveled his shotgun at it.

"Take it easy," Blancanales cautioned. "It's not even alive."

Schwarz lowered his weapon and took a deep breath. "I could have sworn I saw something move in there."

"What's the problem?" Lyons asked.

Schwarz shook his head. "Shadows. Just shadows."

"Yeah, well, shadows can't hurt you," Lyons growled.

But when Schwarz turned to look at the cat again, something did try to hurt him. Five heavy-caliber slugs pounded the wall next to his head, spraying his shoulder and neck with fragments of brick. Gadgets cried out in pain as a dozen tiny cuts opened up beneath his windbreaker and on his face and one hand. "Christ," he muttered, smearing blood on his jeans and picking a particularly nasty fragment out of the back of his hand. "Jesus Christ, what kind of zombies carry M-16s?"

Before anyone could answer, another burst of autofire ripped the darkness, sending Lyons and the others scrambling for cover.

"You all right, Gadgets?" Lyons whispered from the doorway of a doughnut shop.

"No," Schwarz whispered back, wiping more blood from his neck. "I'm not all right. I'm real pissed off." He aimed his Remington at the source of the M-16 fusillade and squeezed off four rounds, as did Blancanales.

Glass shattered and splintered as thin clouds of powdered brick rose into the air and part of the junk shop door blew off. But when Lyons finally ordered the shooting to stop, there was nothing except silence and curling tendrils of mist.

"This is starting to get very freaky," Blancanales said. He peered at the bullet-riddled doorway. "Very fucking freaky."

"Maybe they slipped into that old brothel next to the junk shop," Massard said softly. "Maybe they're inside there waiting for us."

Lyons shook his head. "I don't think so. I think they're right behind us." And sure enough two quick M-16 bursts lanced out from the arcade behind them, pulverizing the brickwork above Lyons's head.

A second burst shattered the window of a cheap hotel and sent Massard and Blancanales scurrying for cover behind a derelict pickup truck. Schwarz, slowed down by his wounds, dropped onto his belly as a dozen 9 mm slugs slammed into the stones around him. He caught a glimpse of another gray figure hovering in the mist, but he couldn't seem to lift his Remington. In fact, he couldn't even lift his hand. He saw glowing eyes like twin emeralds burning in black sockets. He saw lips spreading into a wide smile and an enormous left hand closing around the stock of an M-16. He saw a muzzle aiming for his forehead....

But the shots that were fired weren't from an M-16.

The ghostly figure shivered as the first round from Renny Lussac's .38 slammed into his back. Then, after another two slugs hit him, he staggered out of the swirling mist and gazed at the walls around him. He was a large man, with coarse features and dreadlocks to his shoulders.

"Drop the fucking weapon!" Lussac screamed from the wall above. "Now!"

The assassin grinned, possibly even shrugged. Then, returning his attention to Schwarz, he raised the M-16 and jammed in another magazine.

It was true, Schwarz told himself as the muzzle slowly swung around to fix on his forehead again. You can't kill a zombie. You can't kill a zombie, because they're already dead. You can pump 'em full of slugs till they look like Swiss cheese, but you can't bring them all the way down.

But even as the finality of this thought continued to grow, there were suddenly more shots from the blackness—four long bursts from Carl Lyons's automatic and six deafening cracks from Blancanales's Remington.

And although the zombie remained standing for a moment, his head was gone in a cloud of blood.

Lussac waited at least another twenty seconds before dropping back onto the cobblestones. He waited in the classic pose: weapon extended from his stiff right arm, legs slightly apart, left hand supporting the right wrist. Finally satisfied that the man was dead, he lowered the .38, slid away from the wall and cautiously approached the body.

He examined the contents of the pockets first: one crumpled pack of cigarettes, one book of matches from the Purple Orchid nightclub, three magazines filled with steel-jacketed cartridges, one dime-bag of unidentified white powder. Next he examined the guy's grease-stained Levi's, black sweatshirt, running shoes and bulletproof vest.

As Lussac conducted the examination, the others waited in silence, Schwarz picking fragments of brick from his neck and shoulder, Lyons and Massard kneeling on the damp cobblestones, Blancanales scanning the surrounding doorways.

"Well, at least we've determined that these guys can die," Politician said at last.

Lussac cocked his head and shrugged. "Well, I wouldn't be too sure about that, *cher*. I put four slugs in him back there and he still wouldn't drop. Two slugs in his armpit and two more in his neck ... and I still couldn't bring him down."

Lyons rose to his feet, brushing the soot from his jeans and adjusting his shoulder holster. "So what are you saying, Renny?"

Lussac shook his head. "I'm saying this here boy had something else going for him other than his bulletproof vest. I'm saying he should have dropped dead after the first shot."

"Lot of guys can take a .38 slug without going down, Renny," Massard said. "Why, I've heard of guys who took four or five shots in the head before they collapsed."

Lussac frowned. "Sure, Oz. Sure."

IT WAS NEARLY MIDNIGHT before the forensic boys were finished with the body and the grounds had been swept for clues. Although it had been suggested that Schwarz return to the hospital in order to have his wounds examined, he finally made do with a simple dressing and a few slugs of bourbon from Massard's silver flask. Blancanales was also appreciative of the bourbon.

"So what happens now?" Politician asked between sips from the flask. He was resting on the hood of the ambulance beside Lyons and Lussac. Although the immediate area remained quiet, there were dozens of local residents watching from the windows of the tenements—half-glimpsed eyes peering from behind torn curtains.

"How about we start banging on some doors?" Lyons suggested. "Let's see if we can't find someone around here who's willing to talk to us."

Blancanales nodded and glanced at Lussac. "What do you say, Renny? Any chance some of these people around here will be willing to talk?"

Lussac glanced up at the shadowy faces watching from the windows above, then glanced along the fog-shrouded street where at least another dozen silent figures looked on under the glow of weak street-lamps. Finally he shook his head and sighed. "No, I don't think these people will be willing to talk to us, at least not until we can show them our own brand of magic."

**4**

Within eighteen hours of the shooting below the Richelieu Hotel, a priority cable was dispatched to the Bureau of Alcohol, Tobacco and Firearms. The cable consisted of 122 words and specifically requested that the BATF review their weapons data base for any and all information concerning an M-16 rifle, serial number 42688. Simultaneously the dime bag of unspecified white powder recovered from the body was sent to a laboratory on Commercial Street. Also under analysis at this point were samples of the victim's clothing, hair and blood.

At four o'clock on Wednesday afternoon the information on the various clues was finally assembled. In the interest of comfort and privacy, Lussac and Able Team met for dinner in the garden court of the Napoleon House on Chartres Street. There, over drinks, they carefully examined their clues.

To begin with, Lussac talked about the weapon. Although the piece closely resembled the domestically manufactured model, in fact it had been assembled abroad: the barrel and stock in Thailand, the handgrips in South Korea. Also of interest was the serial number, which indicated the weapon had originally been part of a two-hundred-piece importation from the Dawson Arms Company out of Lexington, Kentucky.

"And this so-called Dawson Arms Company," Lyons asked. "Any indication as to who they are?"

Lussac cocked his head with another easy smile and took a careful sip of his bourbon. "Federal contractor. Definitely a federal contractor."

"Which means what?" Blancanales asked around a mouthful of peanuts. "Military?"

Lussac frowned. "Or else something a little closer to what you might call the heart of darkness."

"Meaning what?" Schwarz asked, his neck and shoulder still studded with tiny cuts.

"Well, let me put it this way," Lussac drawled. "How much do you boys know about the CIA?"

The waiter arrived with huge plates of jambalaya and a local speciality known as muffulett—a large, round loaf of bread filled with various meats and cheese and then smothered in a garlic-drenched olive salad.

"Now, of course, it's still premature to draw conclusions," Lussac said after the waiter put down the plates and departed, "but I think we better start looking at the possibility that our Mr. Baby Shu Duval may add up to a trifle more than the sum of his parts, if you get my drift."

"Yeah, but what would be the point?" Blancanales asked. "I mean, as you said before, why would the Agency want to involve itself with a guy like Duval?"

Lyons picked at his jambalaya. "Actually, I can think of a lot of reasons. Political influence in Haiti, or maybe they just want a piece of the action." He hesitated, then glanced quickly at Lussac. "Then, of course, there's always the possibility that they're playing another one of their psych-ops games."

"Which leads me to point number two," Lussac said, smiling thinly. He then withdrew a slip of paper from the pocket of his linen blazer, spread it on the table and read, "Tetrodotoxin."

"Which is?" Schwarz asked.

"Extract from the puffer fish. Generally a formidable poison, but not in small doses."

"And that's what was in the little bag you found?" Blancanales asked.

Lussac nodded. "Now, once again, it's probably a little premature to draw conclusions, but I'd definitely have to say that it opens up some interesting avenues."

"Such as?" Lyons asked.

"Such as the possibility that we may be facing an army of zombies, after all." Lussac withdrew another slip of paper from the pocket of his blazer, this one covered with scribbled telephone numbers. There were also doodles along the margins of the page: crude drawings of grotesque creatures and a devil in tails and top hat.

"Now you have to understand that I'm not really an expert in these matters," Lussac said after another sip of bourbon. "In fact, you might say I'm just a casual observer. But having spent a little time around the believers, I might be qualified to offer an opinion, for whatever it's worth to you." He speared an olive, then traced a slow finger across the bridge of his nose while keeping his eyes on Lyons and the others. "Now it's just a theory. Remember that."

"Sure," Lyons said. "A theory."

"But it so happens that there are certain people who believe that given a little of that tetrodotoxin stuff, a little bit of faith and a little bit of evil, you can make yourself a real live zombie."

"And by zombie," Schwarz asked, "you mean exactly what?"

Lussac smiled again and popped the olive into his mouth. "The walking dead, my friend."

Up until now the background music had consisted of Mozart selections: a string quartet, one of the early piano sonatas, a few snatches from *The Magic Flute*. Then, without warning, a local blues song called "Happy Superstition" started playing.

"Apparently," Lussac continued, "it was all written up in the medical journals by some doctor from New York City. You give a body just a little bit of that tetrodotoxin and he'll appear to be dead but still retain consciousness. Then you put him in the ground for a while in order to make him think he's dead, then dig him back up and bingo, you've got a guy who actually believes he's a zombie, a guy who'll supposedly do anything for you—anything at all."

"And you actually think Baby Duval is into that kind of stuff?" Lyons asked skeptically.

Lussac popped another olive into his mouth. "Well, I certainly think it's a possibility. I mean, after all, they don't call it voodoo for nothing. Besides, so far we haven't been able to identify any of these victims. Don't you think that's strange? Two bodies, no identification. I think that's very strange, indeed."

Lyons took a deep breath, pushed his plate aside and extracted a toothpick from his pocket. "If you're right, and I'm not saying you are, but *if* you are, then how do you propose we fight him?"

Lussac grinned and rose from the table. "Well, like I said earlier, I think it's time we got ourselves a little of our own *gris-gris*, a little of our own voodoo power."

ANOTHER BAYOU MIST rose with the evening wind, a thin mist that seemed to seep from between the ancient cobblestones and pour out of the gutter drains. At first the air was still sweet with the scent of summer magnolias, but eventually it turned foul again with the stench of mud pools and stagnant water.

For a long time after returning to the Richelieu with Lyons and the others, Lussac had been content to sit by the window while Schwarz continued the investigation by telephone. First, he directed a Stony Man computer search for information about the Dawson Arms Company, then instructed an old friend in the National Security Agency to run a check on federal research programs involving tetrodotoxin. Although the results of his quest were inconclusive, Schwarz did come up with a few interesting details.

"Dawson Arms has definitely done business with the Company," Schwarz told the others.

"What kind of business?" Blancanales asked.

"Mostly small orders for foreign armaments."

"So it's possible Dawson's been supplying Baby Duval with those M-16s, right?" Lyons asked from the opposite corner of the room.

Schwarz nodded. "Yeah. And, as for federally funded research programs involving tetrodotoxin, there are at least three in progress: two conducted by ethnobotanists on behalf of the surgeon general and another possibly conducted inhouse at the CIA's headquarters in Langley, Virginia."

"Any idea why the Company's interested in that stuff?" Blancanales asked.

"Your guess is as good as mine," Schwarz replied.

Finally, after a somewhat veiled telephone call to a casual acquaintance in the DEA, Lyons was able to determine that Baby Shu Duval had indeed been listed as a CIA asset during the spring and summer of 1988. "Low level and arm's length," he told the others, "but definitely CIA."

"Which adds up to what?" Blancanales questioned.

"Voodoo," Lussac whispered from his perch above the garden court. "It all adds up to voodoo."

The thin rivers of mist converging from the alleys and side streets had finally become another awesome fog, while overhead a bloodred moon was perched on the peaked roofs. Explaining to the others that he needed a breath of fresh air, Lyons insisted on accompanying Lussac downstairs to his Chevy. Upon reaching the shadowy courtyard and the flagstone path beneath the cypress trees, they hesitated, watched and listened.

"You feel it, too, don't you?" Lussac asked softly.

Lyons took a deep breath of bayou air and gazed through the filigree of iron lace at the mist in the lane beyond. "Yeah, I guess I do."

"That's how it always begins. First you just sort of feel it, like a sudden chill or a funny tingling along your spine. Then, after a while, you begin to sense them, maybe even hear them calling, *'Gris-gris. Gris-gris. Gris-gris'.*"

"But there's got to be a logical explanation."

Lussac shrugged and fixed his gaze on the deeper shadows between parked cars. "And who's to say voodoo isn't logical? After all, the world's filled with all kinds of strange things science can't explain."

They began to walk again, following the path through the wrought iron gate to the narrow lane between rows of shuttered shops.

"I remember when I was kid," Lussac said, as they neared the corner where he'd left his Chevy. "There was a friend of my mama's who was dying of some sort of intestinal problem. He'd been to all the doctors in town and there was nothing they could do. So finally, in sheer desperation, he consulted what they sometimes call a *houngan*, a kind of voodoo priest. Now this *houngan* was supposed to have had a pretty good rapport with Eshu, the black spirit. So he called down Eshu with a little whisky and a few of the cigars

Eshu likes so much and he asked ol' Mr. Eshu what he was up to. Well, Eshu replied that he was playing a game called making holes, meaning that he had perforated my mama's friend's intestine. So this *houngan* told Eshu to stop making holes or he'd call down Mae de Santo, the mother of all the gods. Well, ol' Eshu didn't want that kind of trouble on his head, so he agreed to leave my mama's friend alone. And the next thing anyone knew, believe it or not, my mama's friend was cured. True story."

Lyons remained silent for a moment, unconsciously fingering the .357 Colt Python pressed against his ribs while his gaze remained fixed on the windshield of Lussac's Chevy. "It could have been a coincidence or sheer willpower."

Lussac eyed Lyons. "Maybe you're right, but you wouldn't have convinced my mama's friend, just like you'll never convince the folks around here that ol' Baby Shu Duval doesn't possess the Power. So you see, it doesn't really matter if it's true or not so long as folks believe it to be true."

"Are you trying to tell me that if we want to enlist the help of this community in terms of witnesses and so forth, we're going to have to consult a *houngan*? Someone who can fight Duval on his own turf?"

Lussac smiled and reached across the hood of his car to retrieve something on the windshield. "Yeah," he said, tossing the chicken claw into the gutter, "that's exactly what I'm saying."

## 5

When Carrie Latrobe was born there were three unmistakable signs that she was destined to speak with the gods. First, there had been a warm, gentle wind that had smelled faintly of the open sea and the islands to the south. Second, the dawn moon had been bone-white and suspended like a wafer on the green horizon. Finally, there had been the birds—three gray doves that remained perched on the telephone wires until the first cry of life. And as if that weren't enough, she couldn't have been a more beautiful child, with raven-black hair like her mother's, the coppery skin of her father and the eyes of someone obviously blessed with the great spirit of *macumba*.

Lyons and Lussac drove out to the edge of the city on Friday to speak with Carrie Latrobe. The house where she lived was a clapboard relic from Victorian times with a drooping porch and rusty screens. Three black children played quietly in the dirt below a spreading magnolia tree. A gray cat with vaguely luminous eyes watched from a dilapidated picket fence.

They found Carrie in the tall grass beside the house with a pile of wet laundry and a basket of clothespins. Although Lussac had told Lyons that she was unusually beautiful, the first vision of her caught the blond warrior entirely off guard. She was an exquisitely slender woman in a yellow dress with a storm of black hair riding her shoulders. She wore no shoes nor jewelry, except for a silver bangle around her left wrist. Supposedly a mulatto with French and Chickasaw blood, she had finely sculpted features, a thin mouth and a delicate nose. Lyons guessed that she was only about twenty-one, but her dark eyes seemed to hold a lot of wisdom.

"I was wondering when you'd come around here," she said as Lussac and Lyons approached.

There was also something about her movements that Lyons found enchanting, something about the cool certainty with which she hung an old cotton shirt on the clothesline, something about the way she brushed a strand of hair from her eyes and inserted a clothespin between her perfect teeth.

"And what made you think I'd be coming around?" Lussac asked in an equally easy drawl.

She shrugged. "Just a feeling, I guess."

Lyons found a seat on an old gray barrel and spotted a second cat, a lean tabby with yellow eyes watching from the deeper weeds.

"This here fellow is a gentleman from the north," Lussac said by way of introduction.

The young woman turned to Lyons, held his gaze for a moment or two, then turned back to the basket of damp clothing. In addition to her own garments, there were blouses and dresses that obviously belonged to a child.

"So what do you want?" she finally asked, reaching for another clothespin.

"I kind of thought it would be obvious, what with all that's been going on around here," Lussac said.

She shrugged again. "Nothing's obvious, Renny Lussac. You ought to know that."

Lussac chewed on a blade of grass and returned the intelligent gaze of the tabby in the weeds. "All right. I guess you could say that we came to seek your professional advice on a sort of unofficial basis."

"Professionally I'm a singer, " she said. "I'm just a singer with a band."

"Well, that isn't what they tell me around Algiers. That isn't what they tell me around Dumaine Street and Congo Square. Around those places you're their priestess, the one who calls down the gods from the sky and opens up the heavens to the faithful."

She brushed another strand of hair from her eyes and glanced up at that dead white sky. Then, turning to face Lussac with a hand on her slender hip, she said, "All right, Renny, how about we try it all over again. Just what is it that you want?"

Lussac ran a finger along the bridge of his nose, meeting her eyes with the shadow of a smile. "I want to talk about Mr. Baby Duval. I want to talk about where he came from, where he's going and how he's going to get there."

"And what makes you think I'd know anything about Mr. Baby Duval?" she asked.

He smiled, rose from the grass and approached. Placing his lips an inch from her ear, he whispered, "Just a feeling."

They adjourned to the house, a dark, cool place with all sorts of odd artifacts heaped around the shabby furniture: crude portraits of jungle saints, a plastic Jesus with a headdress of feathers, a white pony carved from an alligator skull, bottles of what looked like grated bone and blue-green seawater. There was also what might have been some sort of shrine, with a dozen tiny figurines in black wax.

"I'd offer you some coffee," she said, "but all I've got is beer."

"Beer's fine," Lyons replied as he eased himself onto a flowered settee amid a pile of cushions embroidered with the faces of lions and jaguars.

Carrie returned with a plastic tray and two bottles of local brew. When she finally settled into the corner of a sofa, she curled her slender legs beneath her and began to toy with an ostrich feather.

Lussac began with a specific question concerning Duval's influence in the community, but Carrie didn't even bother to answer it. Instead she talked about the larger vision, about the whole notion of spirits among the living and the old gods of Africa.

The first thing that had to be understood, she said, was that *macumba* wasn't a wild cult of the forest. It was a religion, just as Christianity or Judaism was a religion, except for a long time it had only been practiced in secret. The second thing that had to be understood, she said, was that *macumba* had always been a religion of the downtrodden, a religion kept alive by transplanted slaves who whispered the old stories in the night from generation to generation. "And no matter where it's practiced," she added, "the heart of it all still remains in Africa, because that's where the gods dwell."

She picked up a tiny wax figure of a plump child in a grass skirt. "Take this one, for example. His usual name is Ibejis, but everyone calls him Damian. He has a sister named Cosmas, and together they help physicians heal. But a long, long time ago he was also from the jungles of Africa, and so you can only ask him to help with African prayers."

"What about Eshu?" Lussac asked. "Is he from Africa, too?"

She shifted her gaze to the dusty bay window and the long shafts of light that formed milky pools on the carpet. "Eshu is the god of intersections," she said softly. "That's why you always find him at crossroads. But he's also the intermediary between mortals and the greater gods, which is why even good people must sometimes call him down from the sky with whiskey, cigars and blood."

"But we're not talking about good people," Lussac said. "We're not talking about using ol' Eshu as a link to the greater gods. We're talking about using him for himself, about using him as a messenger of death."

She began to trace imaginary circles on the unvarnished coffee table, but her gaze remained distant, fixed. "Of course Eshu is responsible for death. It was his idea. Also inequality, suffering and the hardships of life. All were Eshu's ideas. But he's not completely bad. He's just undisciplined, mischievous and quarrelsome."

"So why do the other gods tolerate him?" Lussac asked.

She smiled enigmatically. "How can they not tolerate him? They need his disorder to counter order. They need him to maintain the delicate balance of things. That's why they put him at the center of things, at the center of space and time. That's why they made him a master of schemes and dark divination." She smiled. "Anyway, I think the other gods find his female aspect amusing in a dangerous sort of way."

Lussac sipped his beer and briefly looked at Lyons. Before he could pose another question, however, the girl began speaking again.

"I know what you're thinking, Renny Lussac. You're thinking that all this *macumba*, all this voodoo stuff, is crazy. You're thinking that the believers are just silly people and that there's nothing to any of these stories about Eshu, who sometimes comes as a devil in a top hat and tails and sometimes as a she demon in silk and veils. You're thinking there's just no truth to any of it."

Lussac shook his head. "No, *chère*, I'm not thinking those things at all. I'm just wondering how a poor boy like me can convince a pretty girl like yourself to help us nail Baby Shu Duval."

Lussac rose to his feet and began a slow tour of the room. Among the artifacts on a bureau in the corner were three African deities in oxidized bronze, but set in an obviously Christian arrangement. There was also a black Jesus and Virgin Mary amid tiny wax lions.

"They tell me you're one powerful priestess," Lussac said at last. "They tell me you're a genuine *mambo* who can pull down the ancient spirits from the sky in order to work your spells."

Carrie shrugged, but still didn't turn her gaze away from the windows. "I can feel and sense things, but I can't always control them."

"Just the same," Lussac said, "if folks around here heard that you were helping us, I kind of think it might make our job a little easier."

She turned and faced the police inspector. "Oh, so that's it. You want me to convince the believers that they have nothing to fear from Baby Duval. You want me to reassure them that they won't be harmed if they put their trust in the police department."

"It's not intended as a trick, *chère*. I just want to even the odds a little, to get a little help on the spiritual end of things. Besides, my mama always said it was important to cover all your bases."

She sighed, shook her head and let her gaze fall to the pools of sunlight. "Baby Shu is very powerful, you know. I think he's probably got himself a very special arrangement with the dark forces, which means it might be impossible for me to intercede."

"Nothing's impossible, *chère*, as long as you put your mind to it."

"All right, then, it would be very dangerous for me to cross Mr. Baby Duval."

Lyons leaned forward, rested his arms on his knees and looked at Carrie. "Mind if I say something, Miss Latrobe?"

She looked at him, but didn't respond.

"Now obviously I don't pretend to know much about all this *macumba* stuff," Lyons continued, "but I do know about guys like Baby Duval. And something tells me you can't afford to do nothing. Something tells me that if you don't take a stand right here and now, then eventually he'll come after you."

"He's right," Lussac added from the opposite corner of the room. "Because, after all, how can Baby hope to consolidate his power in this community of believers as long as there's someone like you to oppose him? I mean, eventually there's going to come a time when he'll have to take you out."

She nodded, but it might have just been a shiver. "You think it's all just the silly delusions of poor, uneducated people, don't you? But the moment I set myself against Mr. Duval, anything can happen, anything at all."

"I know that, *chère*," Lussac replied softly. "I sorely know that. But by the same token, what else can you do?"

After that Lyons and Lussac decided to head back to town. Outside, in the tall grass beneath the trembling cypress trees, the children were still playing silently in the dirt. Although the wind continued to rustle the leaves above, the yard seemed oddly static, the air damp and oppressive.

"They say Baby Duval is the closest thing to pure evil a person can ever meet," Carrie said slowly. "They say he's Satan himself. They also say he has eyes everywhere and that he likes to walk with the wind."

"Well, that may be," Lussac countered, "but I still think we can take him out and send him back to hell if you help us."

At that moment the wind picked up considerably, and they all shivered.

WHILE LYONS AND LUSSAC were speaking with Carrie Latrobe, Schwarz and Blancanales were following a different line of questioning with a man named Woodward Crew.

At about ten-thirty in the morning, Blancanales and Schwarz caught an early shuttle to Tampa, then rented a midnight-blue Thunderbird and proceeded along the causeway into Clearwater. There, after a telephone call to an unlisted number in Langley, they finally found the house—a cavernous estate on the edge of the bay. Supposedly built with Mafia money in the late 1920s, it was a shabby, graying hulk of a place with a wild garden and ivy-laced walls. The broad granite steps were strewn with leaves and snakelike vines. The flagstone path was carpeted with moss, and all sorts of debris lay in the knee-high grass.

Inside, the atmosphere of ancient decay was even more pronounced. The rooms were filled with dark furniture, cracked lampshades and lopsided paintings. A general smell of cats and dry rot mingled with the scent of dead lilacs and roses. Here and there, among the dusty bric-a-brac, were several trophies from Woodward Crew's clandestine career: an iron dagger from Thailand, where Crew had once spent ten months working with rebels in the jungle; a tiny gold stallion from the African Horn, where he'd spent six months attempting to undermine Soviet operations; an ivory cigarette holder from Hong Kong, where he and Blancanales had originally met in the spring of 1972.

Crew was tall and lanky and had the sharp, haughty features of a wealthy New Englander. He wore his gray hair long, though, almost to his shoulders, and his clothing was far from genteel: a Malay wrap over a pair of filthy white trousers. His manners, however, were still impeccable, and he still stocked a pretty good liquor cabinet.

"So," he declared after pouring Schwarz and Blancanales glasses of a twenty-year-old Scotch. "What brings you to my tropical mausoleum?"

"I guess you might say it's a question of old friends and acquaintances," Blancanales replied. "Of connections that can't be ignored."

"I'm retired," Crew said, smiling. "Not semiretired, not lying low and waiting for a better day, not even advising or teaching, but tediously and happily retired."

Blancanales picked up a rusty Russian Revolver lying on a side table. "Remember Charlie Dawson, once a colleague of yours but now the owner of Dawson Arms?''

Crew frowned, then moved to the window, where a thick layer of dust lay on the sill. ''Never liked the guy. Never liked him at all.''

''But you knew him,'' Blancanales said. ''It's in the record. You worked with him for more than twenty months in Haiti.''

Crew shrugged, turned away from the window and drifted back to the liquor cabinet to pour himself a second shot of Scotch. ''Haiti was a bore. Beautiful of course, but basically a bore. Everyone playing six sides against the middle, wondering how to make a buck. Walk into a restaurant and they'd serve you either cats or dogs. And, of course, the natives were always on the verge of revolt. Didn't care much for the weather, either. Too many damn storms.''

''But Charlie liked it, didn't he?'' Blancanales suggested.

''But Charlie was also a bore.'' Crew sighed. ''Brilliant, yes, but a bore.''

''So what was he doing down there?'' Schwarz asked in an effort to steer the conversation onto a more relevant course. ''I mean, apart from the regular Agency bullshit, what was he actually doing there?''

Crew smiled, but primarily to himself. ''Going native. Playing Mr. Kurtz in an absolutely marvelous Conradian fantasy. You know, heart of darkness and all that.''

Crew picked up a photograph album, an old yellowed thing with an embossed floral design and the initials E.C. on the cover. He flipped it open. "This is Charlie," he said with an almost wistful sigh. "This silly-looking fellow right here."

Blancanales extracted the black-and-white snapshot and examined it in the light. It showed a fair-haired man in a tropical suit slouched on the steps of a jungle hut. On his hip he carried a massive .45 revolver, possibly a Webley. Beside him stood an enormous black man holding what looked like an M-16. There was also a dog in the background and a parrot in a bamboo cage.

"I suppose it's a classic story in many respects," Crew said. "Charlie was the great cold warrior out to make the world safe for democracy. They sent him to the Caribbean to win the hearts of the local natives and stop the Red encroachment."

"When was this?" Blancanales asked. "What period are we talking about exactly?"

"The first trip was 1962. Then, following a brief stint back at Langley, they sent him down again in '64."

"What exactly was his mission?" Schwarz asked. "Pacification?"

Crew shook his head with another mouthful of Scotch. "Good God, no. His mission was recruitment and the placement of spies."

"So what went wrong?" Blancanales asked.

Crew smiled thinly. "The jungle began to talk to him. It began to speak to him in a soft but incessant whisper. It described things about him even he didn't know. Things that proved irresistibly fascinating. Things that echoed quite loudly inside his head.''

"We're talking voodoo, right?" Blancanales asked.

Crew nodded. "But not as a believer, exactly. As a manipulator. You see, Charles had this theory. He felt that if you could harness the local belief in voodoo—I mean, really harness it—then you could, in effect, possess the soul of the population."

"So it was really all just a psych-op," Blancanales said. "Dawson goes down to Haiti and sets up his own psychological operation."

Crew nodded again. "I suppose you could say that, at least up to a point."

"And then what happened?" Schwarz prodded gently.

Crew closed his eyes with another dreamy smile. "Then he became obsessed with it all. Totally."

Crew withdrew another cracked and discolored photograph and slid it across the slightly warped coffee table to Blancanales. It showed Dawson seated in the shade of a mango tree with a bottle of beer between his knees and a parrot perched on his shoulder. Beside him, like a shadowy alter ego, was another black man—a corpulent but clearly muscular individual with a hypnotic gaze.

"Duval?" Blancanales asked, tapping the photograph. "Baby Duval?"

Crew poured himself yet another Scotch and downed it with a quick nod. "I suppose, in a sense, you could say Charlie created the man, picked him out of the Port-au-Prince gutters and shaped him into a dark god, a dark prince of voodoo the likes of which no one had ever seen before.''

"But why?" Schwarz asked.

Crew shrugged. "Partly to prove it could be done, I suppose, and partly for the operational benefits.''

"Which were?" asked Blancanales.

"Well, control for one thing. After all, voodoo is a significant religion on the island. Thus, if you could control the believers by controlling a dominant leader, you could control the whole society. Or so Charlie believed.''

"And did it work?"

"Like a bloody charm.''

After that Crew invited his guests to stay on for lunch, but Blancanales said they had to get back to New Orleans. On their way down the leaf-strewn steps of the old house, Crew said, "By the way, you never actually told me what this is all about. Not that I mean to pry, of course.''

"It's about Duval," Blancanales replied sharply. "He's surfaced again.''

"In the Big Easy?"

"That's right.''

Crew digested this information for a long time, then ran a hand across his sunburned face. "Well, I suppose that was bound to happen sooner or later.''

"Why do you say that?" Schwarz asked.

"Because Baby Shu was never one to fade into obscurity, not after what Charlie Dawson did for him.''

"What do you mean?" asked Blancanales.

"Well, as I said, Charlie turned Duval into a god. He gave him an illusion of power such as can only be imagined. And like all false gods, Baby was the first to believe in himself."

"There's also some indication that Duval is into coke and other nasty things," Schwarz said.

Crew nodded. "Yes, well, that would constitute his economic power base, you see. But if you want to stop the bastard, I'm afraid you'll have to meet him on his own ground. You'll have to destroy his reputation of invincibility among his followers."

"And how would you suggest we do that?" asked Blancanales.

Crew sighed. "I'm not sure, actually. But I will tell you one thing. It's not necessarily all just an illusion."

"What do you mean?" Schwarz asked, suddenly growing very serious, his eyes fixed on Crew's profile.

"I mean that although much of Duval's power probably stems from an elaborate ruse, I wouldn't entirely discount the supernatural aspect. Because, you see, there really is something to this voodoo stuff. I'd take it a little more seriously if I were you."

BLANCANALES AND SCHWARZ returned to New Orleans in the early evening, and met with Lyons and Lussac at the Richelieu Hotel. The sky was still cloudy, the air still warm and heavy. Although Schwarz attempted to lighten things up with a joke or two, the mood remained uneasy. Blancanales complained of a headache. Lyons had developed a rash on his left wrist. Lussac kept gazing off into empty space and nervously drumming his fingers on a table. The repetitious cries of birds in the cypress trees got on everyone's nerves.

Finally, after padding off to the minibar in search of a beer, Schwarz heard screaming from the adjoining room. A moment later four rapid shots were fired. When Lyons and the others rushed into the room, they found Schwarz standing in the corner, his eyes fixed on the telephone cord. There were four blackened holes in the shag rug and the cord had been severed in two places.

"Don't even say it," Schwarz snapped. "Just don't even fucking say it."

Lyons stared at him. "What happened?"

"I thought it was a snake, okay? I was reaching for a beer and I thought I saw a snake move out of the corner of my eye."

Blancanales smiled. "So you killed the telephone cord?"

Schwarz smirked. "Yeah, so I killed the telephone cord."

But no one really felt like laughing. Someone or something else did that from deep within the walls.

6

Although Carrie had always called the old man Uncle John, he was actually no one's uncle.

It was late, well past midnight, and the fog had risen again, pouring out of the cypress groves and moving like a slow flood across the railroad tracks to the edge of the old man's cottage. Occasionally an owl hooted from the edge of the swamp, but mainly it was silent except for the regular throb of crickets.

"Every dog has his day," the old man whispered.

Carrie placed her hand in the old man's, shut her eyes and let her head drop onto his knee. Like many of the Great Spirit priests, the old man was a legendary figure—a thin, shadowy black man from nowhere, a bent gray ghost of a man with no real family, home or past. Carrie couldn't recall where and how she had met him. He had simply always been there, originally drawn to her by the signs, then later out of love. Although there had been weeks when she didn't see him, he was always there.

"I'm scared, Uncle John," she whispered.

The old man bent to plant a gentle kiss on her forehead. "Oh no, child. Oh, no. All you got to do is remember that every little dog has his day and that this just happens to be Baby Shu's day. But sooner or later it's going to pass.''

She lifted her head and gazed at the outline of various objects around her. There was an old porcelain vase filled with dried willows, four strawberry jam bottles filled with a liquid that seemed to glow in the darkness, the petrified hand of a hanged thief, and the bleached skull of a Choctaw warrior.

''They want me to fight him,'' she said at last. ''That's the part I didn't tell you, Uncle John. Renny Lussac wants me to fight Baby Duval so that folks won't be scared of him. He wants people to stand up as witnesses.''

The old man nodded and gently shifted in his rocker. ''Well, that's all right, child. You can fight him good and clean.''

''But how?''

The old man smiled and let his hand drop to her shoulder. ''Well, first thing you got to do is believe, child. No matter what happens, you got to keep believing in the power of the spirits above. Then you got to get your satchel of powerful things and make your little offerings in order to let the spirits know you're pure of heart and mind. Then you whisper a little prayer or two in order to let them know exactly what you want. And if that don't work, you shout at 'em.''

''But what if they don't listen to me? What if they only hear Baby Duval?''

''Then you shout louder. You shout and make them listen.''

Dogs began to howl from beyond the cypress groves and the wind moved through the grass. Then, very suddenly, there was nothing, not even the throb of crickets.

"He's out there, isn't he?" she whispered. "He's out there walking around again."

The old man nodded, but didn't seem very concerned. "That's right, child. Ol' Baby Shu and his slaves are out walking around again."

"What if they come here before I'm ready?"

The old man smiled and shook his head. "No, child, they're not walking for you. They be walking for Monsieur Renny Lussac and them three Yankees of his. That's who they be walking for tonight."

"Then shouldn't we warn them?"

The old man shook his head again. "No, child, there ain't nothing we can do. But that don't mean you should be worrying, either, because that ol' Renny Lussac has got some fine style, and those Yankees also be plenty strong. Strong, indeed."

AT THAT MOMENT, however, Lyons didn't feel particularly strong. He felt drained and listless in the aftermath of a dream in which he saw himself slowly bleeding to death with a knife between his shoulder blades.

He propped himself on an elbow, threw back the sweat-drenched sheets and glanced at his wristwatch. It was four o'clock, the dead hour. He groped in the darkness for the glass of water on the nightstand, took a long sip, then spit out something soft and vile that must have been floating on the surface. A moth? He shook his head, sagged back against the pillow and shifted his gaze to the gently billowing curtains. Ghosts?

It was crazy, he told himself, completely crazy. Sure, Duval might have something going for him, but it had nothing to do with black magic. It was simply a matter of psych-ops, carefully planned and beautifully orchestrated.

He propped himself on his elbows again and looked at the slowly shifting shadows that flickered on the far wall. Apart from the wind, he could hear a cat stalking through the grass. Or was it a cat?

There were no ghosts, zombies or disembodied fiends shifting on the breeze, he told himself. There were only bad dreams and hallucinations.

He tossed back the sheets again, took a deep breath of sultry air and swung himself out of bed. He shouldn't have had that last drink, he chastised himself. Or that damn pizza. He got to his feet, briefly shut his eyes with a sudden wave of nausea and caught a quick image from his nightmare: a black hulk of a man approaching out of the shadows with a knife the size of a pool cue. Damn anchovies, he cursed.

Adjusting his boxer shorts on his hips, he stepped out on the balcony and moved to the railing. Although the garden below was motionless, there were all kinds of shifting shadows among the coils of vines and vegetables.

But when Lyons began spinning to the left and dropping into a crouch, he wasn't just jumping at

shadows. He'd caught a glimpse of a heavy black man
with a bare torso, bare feet and a pair of old dunga-
rees secured at the waist with a length rope. And he'd
caught a whiff of the stench, the vaguely sweet stink
of rotting flesh. Then, spinning off the railing to avoid
the slashing knife, he saw the half-decayed face
swarming with maggots.

Lyons backed up against the wall, feeling the rough
stucco prick his naked back. Although the knife
wasn't as long as the one he'd seen in his dream, it was
long enough—at least eighteen inches of glistening
stainless steel.

He feinted with his shoulder but the creature simply looked at him and grinned, revealing an inch of
naked bone along the jaw. There were also raw ten-
dons visible along the thing's throat, and what looked
like a gaping bullet hole in the side of his head.

*I still don't believe in you,* Lyons whispered to himself. *I don't believe you're anything more than a
cleverly constructed trick from a psych-op factory.*

But when the knife flashed again, he had to believe
in the pain. As he spun to the left, he winced and
looked in dismay at the blood issuing from his chest.
The thing grinned malevolently at him. Believe it or
not, he was in trouble. It was time to show the fiend
in front of him what a good commando could do.

He lashed out with a snap kick, careful to keep his
toes back so that the impact was made with the ball of
his foot. The blow hit the brute's groin like a sledge-
hammer, and Lyons watched with relief as the creature's eyes grew wide with pain and his jaw dropped.

Before his attacker could regroup, Lyons whipped an elbow into the man's face.

Warm blood sprayed from the black man's nose and mouth, proving that the bastard wasn't some half-decayed corpse. He was human, all right.

Lyons struck a third time with a fist to the groin and felt another hot spray of saliva and blood. Then, clamping the knife hand under his elbow and turning with a quick pivot, he jammed the arm across his knee until he heard the bone crack.

The black man screamed loud enough to rattle the windows. And he shrieked again as Lyons twisted back the fractured arm to wrench the knife free. Quickly Lyons plunged the blade into the crumpling assassin's rib cage.

They clung to each other for a few more seconds, then, by degrees, Lyons felt the monster's grip falter, the enormous hands slowly slip away. When the zombie killer fell, he seemed to collapse in stages—first to his knees, then to all fours, and finally out for the count.

Lyons also sank to his knees. He reached for the knife and gradually withdrew it from the black man's belly. Nothing special, just your everyday carving knife, the kind you'd find in every well-stocked kitchen. He took another deep breath, inhaling the sickeningly sweet stench of rancid meat, and examined the blade. Real blood, all right. He shut his eyes, shivering slightly with the breeze. Then, slowly extending the tip of the blade, he gently prodded the rotting flesh around the face. The maggots didn't move, and the skin fell away like clay...or theatrical makeup. He extended the blade again, gently prodding and digging until he managed to remove a bit of the horribly exposed bone. It was plastic, beautifully shaped and perfectly tinted plastic.

CARRIE OPENED HER EYES, lifted her head from the old man's knee and gazed dully at the room around her. Although nothing had obviously changed, something was very different.

"What happened?" she whispered. "Uncle John, what happened?"

The old man also opened his eyes and looked around the room. "Nothing happened, child. Nothing except that maybe our ol' Mr. Baby Shu Duval just lost himself one of his zombies."

Carrie glanced at the billowing curtains and caught a dim view of shifting cypress boughs through the window. Although the owl had grown silent, the throb of the crickets had resumed.

"But how do you know?" she asked. "How can you be so sure?"

The old man smiled and let his hand drop gently onto her shoulder. "I just know, child. I just shut my eyes and move on out into the cool, cool night, and then I know."

"But how did it happen? I mean, if zombies are already dead, then how can they be killed?"

"Like I told you, child, them Yankee friends of Mr. Renny Lussac might not be believers, but they're powerful. Real powerful."

"Well, then maybe they won't need me. Maybe they can fight Baby Duval on their own."

The old man smiled again, then slowly shook his head. "No, child, they're going to need you. Sooner or later they're going to need you real bad."

## 7

According to the boys from forensics, the carving knife recovered from the body on the terrace of the Richelieu Hotel had been manufactured by Proud Eagle Cutlery in Cleveland. It was made of stainless steel, usually sold for about fifteen dollars and was available in virtually every department store in the U.S. In other words, it constituted a very thin lead.

As for the identity of the man who had wielded the knife, once again forensics drew a blank. The perp had either never existed in the first place or else had undergone one hell of an identity erasure—fingerprints, dental, everything.

The theatrical makeup removed from the black man's face, however, offered a more promising lead. Manufactured by the Clare Anderson Company in Hollywood, it was generally only available through professional cosmetology outlets. Locally there were only two such distributors. One on Bourbon Street and another called Stage and Beauty Supply between Polydras and Commercial Streets.

Just after ten o'clock in the morning, Renny Lussac returned from Stage and Beauty Supply to meet

Lyons and the others on the patio of a coffeehouse at the edge of Jackson Square. In contrast to the previous day, the sky was clear with balmy winds from the Gulf. Although Lyons hadn't required stitches for the knife slash across his chest, he still found the butterfly bandages restrictive. He was also still bone-tired.

"So?" Lyons asked as Lussac sat down with his doughnuts and coffee.

The police inspector lifted his eyebrows. "So what?"

"So what happened at Stage and Beauty Supply?"

"Ah," Lussac replied, dropping a morsel of doughnut into his mouth. "Well, let me tell you, there are some very strange folks in this town."

"Meaning specifically?" Blancanales asked.

Lussac withdrew a worn business card, glanced at the name, and then used it to pick his teeth. "Well, take the proprietor of Stage and Beauty Supply, for example. Quite apart from the fact that he's a little light in his loafers, he seems to have an overactive imagination. For instance, when I asked him who purchased the theatrical makeup in question, he kept insisting that it was none other than an emissary of the Devil himself. Now what do you make of that?"

Schwarz shrugged, then smiled. "Did you get an address?"

JUST BELOW DUMAINE STREET, between North Rampart and Beauregard Square stood an especially shabby block of tenements that were sometimes called the Congo Caves. Even the guidebooks advised travelers to stay clear of the neighborhood, and local residents knew better than to linger outside after dark. Among other things, it was said that the Congo Caves had once been the home of grave robbers, shadowy ghouls who dug up corpses and sold them to the voodoo priests. It was also around here that one Charlotte Leblanc was said to have hacked up her daddy with an ax, and one Alvin Toe was said to have murdered sixteen black boys and served them up in a gumbo stew. More recently it was also said that Baby Duval had recruited some of his most loyal followers from the caves, including an emaciated junkie who called himself Leon Mozart.

Around six o'clock in the evening Lussac led Able Team into the neighborhood. Although a small crowd still lingered in the square where a desultory band played for small change, the side streets were mostly deserted. Here and there a prostitute posed in a darkened doorway, while a pimp watched from the window above. But mostly the residents had moved inside when the fog rose.

From the outside the Caves looked like any of the neighboring apartment blocks. It had a crumbling stucco facade with a filigree of iron in a Spanish motif. Inside, however, the caves looked like a little slice of hell. The walls were tattooed with the worst imaginable graffiti: leering devils in red spray paint, smirking vampires in black, crude outlines of mutilated bodies and every conceivable obscenity. Also, in what must have been a fit of perverse inspiration, someone had written: "Baby Shu is in my head now that he's brought me back from the dead."

"Just in case he gets a little nervous and tries to bolt," Lussac said to Blancanales, "maybe you and Gadgets better wait here in the lobby."

Blancanales drew his .357 Colt Python from his shoulder holster and slipped it into the folds of his windbreaker. "How do you want us to play it if he starts shooting?" he asked.

Lyons glanced at Lussac, who had also withdrawn his .38 Police Special. "Play it any way you have to," he said. "Though I don't imagine I have to tell you that he's our best lead so far. We wouldn't want to waste him, would we?"

Beyond the lobby was an equally shabby corridor, then a flight of concrete stairs to an unlighted hallway. Among the more grotesque drawings spray painted on the second-floor walls was a hanged man with a needle protruding from his throat. There was also a dead cat at the top of the stairs, probably the victim of someone's minor revenge.

According to the mail slot downstairs, Leon Mozart lived in apartment 22 at the top of the stairs. The faint rhythm of conga drums echoed from within the room.

Lussac and Lyons drew their weapons and pressed themselves against the walls on either side of the door. Then, extending a fist and knocking, Lussac shouted, "Police, Leon baby! Police!"

There was nothing but silence, and what might have been the sound of a shotgun being cocked.

"You hear me, Leon? Open the goddamn door!"

Another eight or nine seconds of silence passed, broken only by what might have been the noise of a shell sliding into a chamber.

"Come on, Leon. I know you're in there. Open the damn door or we'll bust it down. Do you hear me, Leon?"

"I hear you fine," Mozart said as he squeezed off the first shot.

Lussac had been reaching for the brass doorknob when the panel exploded in a shower of splinters. Lyons, crouched against the opposite wall, dropped to one knee but couldn't get a clear shot until Mozart's twelve-gauge exploded again, leaving only pieces of the door swinging on the hinges. Then, leaping through the threshold with his Colt Python leveled at Mozart's head, Lyons shouted, "Don't even breathe, pal!"

Mozart dropped the shotgun as if it were red-hot.

"Take a load off your feet, Leon," Lussac growled, as he shoved the thin, dreadlocked mulatto into a straight-backed chair. "We got a lot to talk about and I see no reason why you shouldn't relax."

Mozart eyed Lussac uneasily, then folded his arms across his chest and smiled. "What about my rights, huh?"

"You waived your rights, Leon, my friend, when you tried to blow our heads off," Lussac replied. "Besides, rights apply to human beings, not zombies."

"Maybe I should just break his arm," Lyons said as he sifted through a box of electrical components. Mozart's room was crammed with all kinds of stolen goods. "Maybe I should break his arm and pull out the bone."

Lussac shook his head. "Too messy. I think we should just hook him up to the light socket and fry his dick."

Leon had obviously played this game before. He just kept smiling.

Finally, after sifting through a drawer filled with filthy socks and torn underwear, Lussac found what he was looking for: two tiny wax images of Eshu, the god of intersections.

"Okay, Leon," Lussac said softly, "how about we get down to business? Let's stop beating around the bush and start talking about what's really going on."

Mozart glanced at the skull in Lussac's hand, then turned his eyes to the wall. "I don't know what you're talkin' about, man. They just some ol' things I found layin' around in the basement, that's all."

"In the basement, huh?" Lussac said. "Whose basement? Baby Shu Duval's?"

Mozart shook his head, but couldn't seem to form his lips into a word.

"Well, how about I help you?" Lussac said softly. "How about I tell you what these things are all about? These things are about voodoo, about catching souls and feeding them to the Devil. Isn't that right?"

Mozart's eyes began to roll back into his head and his left hand shivered with a tiny spasm. "Look, I don't know nothin' about all that,'' he moaned. ''I don't know nothin' about no Baby Shu Duval.''

''Yeah? Well, that's not what I heard. I heard you and Baby are real close. In fact, I heard you and Mr. Baby Duval are so close that he even trusts you with the purchase of certain very special magical potions, such as you might buy at Stage and Beauty Supply downtown.''

Mozart shivered again, and beads of perspiration erupted on his forehead. ''Okay, so maybe every once in a while I do a favor for Baby Shu. Maybe he tells me to go buy him somethin' and then maybe I do it. Where's the crime in that, huh? I mean, I just do little things for him, okay? It ain't no big deal.''

''What's the makeup for?'' Lussac asked.

Mozart shrugged. ''It's just a joke, right? Because Baby Shu, he's supposed to be able to, you know, turn dudes into zombies. He's supposed to, you know, give them this powder and maybe sometimes even bury them alive so he can raise them from the dead to, you know, do his biddin'. But it's all just a joke, man. I mean, like he can't really raise a dude from the dead. The makeup is just so they look like they been raised from the dead.''

''Who's idea was it?'' Lyons asked with menace in his voice. ''Who had the idea to use the makeup?''

A shadow briefly clouded Mozart's eyes, but he managed to shake it off. ''I dunno, man. I guess it was Baby's idea. I mean, he's always gettin' these ideas. He just puts his mind to somethin', and all of sudden he has a flash of inspiration. But it ain't no magic. It ain't no voodoo. It's just a scam."

Lussac moved away from where Mozart sat and drifted across the room, casually inspecting a pile of obviously stolen appliances. In addition to the usual toasters and microwave ovens, there was a compact disk player and a VCR. "You're still on probation, aren't you?"

Mozart shrugged. "So?"

"So you got receipts for all this stuff?"

Mozart stuck out his jaw in a gesture of absurd defiance. "What do I need receipts for? Them things were gifts from my sister in New York City."

Lussac picked up the compact disk player for a closer examination. "Know something, Leon? I bet if I were to run this here serial number, I'd find this CD player was stolen."

Mozart glanced at Lyons, saw not even a trace of sympathy, then looked up at the water-stained ceiling. "Okay, so maybe I didn't get them from my sister. Maybe they was gifts from my cousin."

"What cousin?"

"My cousin, ah, Jackson. Yeah. Maybe they was gifts from my cousin Jackson, and maybe he was the one who stole 'em. He's always had a problem with things like that. Know what I mean?"

Lussac shook his head and smirked. "Way I see it, Leon, is that you're going to be doing some more time. You're going to be stuck back in the slammer for at least another three or four years. And just so we make sure you're rehabilitated, I'm going to personally ask that you be kept away from anything even faintly resembling a high. Know what I mean?''

Suddenly Mozart stiffened, and his eyes went dead for a moment.

"How about it, Leon?" Lussac asked. "Do you want to spend the next few years completely cold turkey? Do you like the idea of waking up behind bars with every nerve in your body screaming for a fix? Is that the way you want to play it?''

Finally snapping the invisible cables that held him rigid, Mozart slumped a little lower his chair. "All right,'' he groaned, "what do you want to know?''

Lussac drifted back to position himself beside Mozart's chair, withdrew a pack of Camels and stuck one between the thief's lips. "Tell me about Baby Duval. Tell me what he's got going around here.''

Mozart nodded, then said, "Look, I only seen him a few times, right? Maybe three, four times all told.''

"Where?''

"Different places.''

"Such as?''

"Such as an ol' warehouse in Storyville and a wharf down by the river. But mostly they say he hangs out in some place outside of town where I never been. I just heard about it.''

"What else do you hear?''

"He can do things.''

"What kind of things?''

"Bad things, real bad things. Even though he sometimes uses tricks and stuff to, you know, spice up his act a little, that don't mean he ain't got the power.''

"Yeah? And what exactly does he do with this power?"

"Lots of things, man. Like maybe he'll enter your dreams so he can mess with your head. Or maybe he'll cause you to go crazy. Or maybe he'll even make you die so he can turn you into a zombie."

"Yeah? Well, I thought you said there were no zombies, Leon. I thought you said it was all just a scam."

"Well, I was lyin'. Because they're out there. Baby Shu, he might make 'em more ugly with makeup and stuff, but that don't mean they're not the walkin' dead. And maybe Baby Shu sometimes does tricks he picked up from this dude in the north, but that don't mean he can't catch your soul, put it in a jar and make you do his biddin' for the rest of eternity."

Lussac exchanged a quick glance with Lyons, then got to his feet and withdrew another cigarette. Although his eyes were fixed on the neon sign blinking across the street, his voice remained steady and determined. "What dude from the north?"

Mozart responded with a blank look. His eyes were now riveted on the flashing neon at the Isabelle Bar and Grill, too. "Huh?"

"You said Baby Shu sometimes resorts to various tricks he picked up from this dude in the north. Well, I'm asking you to tell me about that dude."

Another flood of perspiration broke out on Mozart's face, leaving long tracks across his cheeks. "Look, man, I can't just—"

"The dude from the north," Lussac repeated. "Who is he, Leon?"

"He's just this dude, man. An older dude."

"What's he look like?"

"I don't know. He's a white guy. A middle-aged white guy."

"And what's his relationship with Baby Duval?"

"Say what?"

"What does he do for Baby Duval?"

"He don't do nothin' for him. He just sort of offers advice. He tells Baby Shu how to, you know, influence people, how to make 'em believe in him and respect him."

"Does this northern dude happen to have a name?" Lyons asked.

Mozart ran a hand across his forehead, then stared at his glistening palm for a moment. "Mr. D. Everybody just calls him Mr. D."

"And where does this Mr. D. come from?" Lussac asked.

"I told you," Mozart moaned. "From the north."

"Yeah, but where in the north?" Lyons pressed. "It's a big place."

Mozart shook his head and glanced at the window again.

"Where?" Lussac snarled. "Where exactly does Mr. D come from?"

"Look, man, I wasn't kiddin' when I said Baby Duval has got himself some kind of bad power. I mean, he can do things to me. He can come around here at night and do terrible things to me."

"So can we, Leon," Lussac growled. "Spill it. Where does Duval's friend come from?"

Although Mozart nodded his head, there was once again something wrong with his eyes, something that kept them glued to the window as his left hand started to tremble and his right leg spasmed.

"Where?" Lussac repeated.

Then, although Mozart might have whispered something—a name, place, something—it was lost in the clatter of the toppling chair and the flurry of his escape.

Lyons responded first, whirling from the corner and diving for Mozart's legs. But by the time he had crossed the gap of three feet, Mozart was already midway to the window. Lussac responded next with a desperate lunge and even managed to grab hold of Mozart's T-shirt. But the raging intensity of Mozart's rush was simply too much, and as the T-shirt ripped, all Lussac could do was shout, "No!"

Mozart seemed to hesitate before he leaped, a brief moment of hesitation while his body coiled like a spring. Then, screaming again, he plunged through the curtain and into the empty space beyond.

Lussac got to his feet slowly and moved to the window beside Lyons. There were fragments of glass out there, traces of blood, but other than that it seemed as if nothing had really changed. Then, little by little, thanks to the blinking neon of the Isabelle Bar and Grill, he was able to make out a tortured shape impaled on the wrought-iron spikes that topped the gates below. "Kind of makes you wonder, don't it?" he muttered.

Lyons slumped against the filthy plaster, then looked down at the impaled body. "Makes you wonder about what?"

"Evil," Lussac said. "About evil."

## 8

It must have been about four o'clock in the afternoon when Carrie first sensed Baby's presence. Earlier the day had been problematic in a number of respects. The air had been so moist and static that the laundry hadn't dried. The neighbor's child had stepped on a nail, and the mail brought bills that she couldn't pay. Toward noon she discovered an infestation of fire ants in her cupboards and a dead frog floating just below the surface of her wash basin.

But by four o'clock in the afternoon it wasn't just a matter of signs, she also felt it. Felt it in every fiber of her body: Duval.

For a long time after sensing Baby's presence, Carrie remained in her parlor seated among her satchels of *gris-gris*, icons and relics. Then, finally fixing on the drone of an enormous horsefly, she picked up a satchel of *gris-gris* and moved out along the path between the glistening cypress trees.

There were several holy places where she could make her stand: the Riverbend Temple by the docks, which was known to be particularly attractive to the spirits of luck, the Temple of Ramparts, which was conducive to the spirits of healing; and the main *hounfor*, or temple, in the French Quarter, where the spirits were known to be especially kind to those in danger. In the end, however, she chose the Place of Waters, where she had been born.

There had always been something reassuring about the Place of Waters, something about the faint glow of afternoon light through the foliage and the whisper of overhead leaves, that had always filled her with a sense of security. It was here, for example, that Uncle John had first explained the secrets of the *loa*, the primary divinities of voodoo belief. It was here that she had witnessed her first descent of spirits, felt them entering her body and rejoiced in the pulse of her blood. Finally, it was here that she had come to pray for her mother's soul.

Although the Place of Waters was ostensibly no different than a hundred undeveloped coves along the farther reaches of the Mississippi tributaries, she generally felt the power even before she actually entered the grove. This was hallowed ground, a terminal to heaven. This was Africa, the land of her ancestors.

She entered the grove slowly, letting her eyes naturally follow the curve of the shore. Despite the outline of derricks above the distant willows, the Place of Waters was still quite a beautiful place. There were tiger lilies the size of basketballs, logs beneath the water's surface that seemed to glow like Christmas decorations, stiff-winged kingfishers, gently cooing doves and the occasional alligator.

She knelt in the grass to unpack her satchel. Although Uncle John had always maintained that her strength lay with the spirit of love, today she would invoke Oxum—the Saint of War. To this end, she had brought three white candles, a flask of whiskey, a bag of uncooked rice and a side of salted pork. Although she knew he favored fresh meat, a fresh kill, she hoped the pork would do. Also, she hadn't been able to locate his armor and sword, so she would have to make do with a tortoise shell and a kitchen knife.

She sang as she began to place these objects on the grass, an old song that Uncle John had taught her. Although her voice sounded pitifully thin among the towering trees and motionless willows, she felt confident that Oxum was listening. After all, he might be the god of war, but he was also the protector of innocence.

She shut her eyes and allowed herself a little smile as a breeze finally began to stir through the willows. Bowing her head, she whispered a prayer of thanks when she thought she heard the warrior's footsteps treading softly through the grass. But when she opened her eyes and glanced over her shoulder, she saw that it wasn't Oxum.

She put down the candle and the slice of salted pork. Although the tall man who watched from the shadows still hadn't shown his face, she was fairly certain she recognized him from the *hounfor* near Congo Square. His name was Louis Dulac, and he was related to a woman who lived not far from Uncle John.

Then, as a slow chill rose from the base of her spine and the blood drained slowly from her face, she also remembered that he had died of a sudden and mysterious illness more than six months ago.

She pulled herself to her feet and took a slow step backward. "Louis?" she called softly. "Is that you, Louis?"

The man slid out of the shadows to reveal a bony face, thin shoulders and coils of gray-black hair. Although his feet were bare and his trousers soiled with mud, his coat was obviously the finest he had ever owned—the coat they had buried him in.

"Louis?" she whispered again. Then marginally louder, "Louis, is that you?"

"Yes," he rasped in a voice that clearly wasn't his own. "It's me."

She took another step back toward the water, feeling her bare feet sink into the soft ground. "What do you want?" she asked, hoping to buy a little time.

"What do I want?" he rasped with a toothy grin. "What do I want? Why, I want what my master has told me to want—*you!*"

She took another step toward the water, then glanced at the path that skirted the marsh. There were homes beyond those trees, she thought vaguely, homes of believers who would help her. But before she could even begin to take another step, he was virtually on top of her.

"Don't be afraid," he cooed. "Don't you be afraid at all. My master, he don't want to hurt you. He just want to be with you, to love you, to make you his own.''

He caught her by the arm and threw her to the grass. Then, grabbing a handful of her hair to pin her down, he tore a long strip of thin cotton from her dress.

She looked at him, her nostrils flaring, arms across her breasts, legs drawn up to her chin. ''Don't do this,'' she whispered. ''This is wrong. Do you understand, Louis? It's wrong.''

He smiled, extended a hand to her throat and slowly traced the curve of her shoulder. Then, in a voice that seemed to resonate from deep within the pit of his stomach, he said, ''I'm not Louis, Miss Carrie. I'm not Louis Dulac no more.''

She cried out as he fell on her, cried out to the gray sky above and the ring of trembling cypress trees. Then, for a moment, she remained quite still and silent, turning away from his fetid breath and the stench of death oozing from his body. She recalled he had always been a sickly man, but now he was incredibly strong, stronger than she would have ever dreamed possible. And there was something wrong with his eyes, something about the way the pupils expanded even when he stared at the light.

She cried out again as he pried her legs apart and ran his hand along her thigh, hip and left breast.

''This is nice,'' he cooed. ''This is real nice.''

She felt his lips on her neck, his teeth gently nibbling the veins along her throat.

''Real nice,'' he murmured. ''Real, real nice.''

She shut her eyes again, mechanically whispering her song to Oxum. Of course, he couldn't possibly hear her now, not above the grunt of the monster attacking. Nevertheless, she kept on whispering to him over and over again.

Then she caught another glimpse of her rapist's eyes, eyes that seemed to contain the bleakest landscape she'd ever seen. It was a truly horrible place of cracked plains and stony crags, the birthplace of nightmares, a land as old as Africa itself, as old as hell.

She felt his hand on her breast again, slowly kneading the flesh with filthy fingers. He was telling the truth, she thought vaguely. He wasn't Louis. He was Baby Shu possessed by Eshu the Terrible.

"Yeah," the creature breathed, meeting her horrified gaze and grinning again. "Now you understand, don't you darlin'?"

But suddenly all she really knew was that he was about to enter her, to own her as completely as he owned his half-dead slaves. And in that moment of absolute revulsion, she cried out again for Oxum.

When he finally came, he came with the wind, a strangely warm wind that seemed to rise up from nowhere, roaring through the surrounding leaves and sweeping across the grass like a tiny storm.

Oxum of the Sword, patron saint of ancient battles.

She felt him filling her with his breath, a long, slow breath that surged through her limbs with unimaginable power.

Oxum of the Shield, patron saint of warriors.

She shut her eyes again as her rapist wedged himself between her thighs. She arched her back as he grabbed another handful of hair. But when he finally yanked down his trousers, she let the spirit ride.

She struck out with the side of her left hand, a blind blow delivered with more force than she ever thought possible. It caught her rapist across the jaw and left him momentarily stunned. Then, suddenly meeting his gaze again, letting him see for himself the power of Oxum, she hit him full in the face.

The rapist recoiled with a mouthful of blood, collapsed on his hands and knees, then stared at her again. "You," he rasped. *"You!"*

She met his gaze directly, letting him enter through her eyes so that he could also feel the power of Oxum.

"Yes," she replied in a ringing voice. *"Me!"*

He charged from a half crouch, springing as the wind rose again through bending cypress boughs. She saw his pupils widen as if his eyes were about to burst. She saw his lips draw back to reveal yellowed teeth. She saw his face contort in a furious rage, then felt him churning with a series of quick transformations: Louis to Baby, Baby to Eshu.

But by this time she also felt her fingers closing around the handle of the kitchen knife in the grass, felt the warm breeze filling her shoulders and arms as she brought the knife into play. Then she felt his body working against the blade, his blood seeping along her wrist and arm, his last hot breath on her face.

He seemed to take a long time to die. Through it all he continued to stare at her, first as the sneering Eshu, then as the grinning Duval and finally, pitifully, as a thoroughly confused Louis Dulac.

For a long time she just knelt in the grass, feeling the warm breath of power flowing out of her lungs and into the surrounding leaves. Her tears also felt warm, but the knife in her hand had grown terribly cold.

"I'M SORRY," Schwarz said, "but I just don't buy it."

He was standing on the balcony, resting his weight on the railing and gazing down at the darkening outline of magnolias and roses in the hotel garden below. It was just after seven in the evening, and the last glow of sunlight still lingered on the rooftops while the first strains of steel guitars wafted up from the basement clubs.

Lyons pried open a beer and slid it into Schwarz's hand. Through the French doors behind him, Lussac spoke softly on the telephone while Blancanales tried to comfort Carrie Latrobe.

"Nobody's asking you to believe anything," Lyons said. "I'm just saying that maybe you should hear what they have to say."

"Hear what they have to say about what?" Schwarz countered with a smirk. "Girl walks in covered with blood, says she just killed a guy who died six months ago, except she didn't really kill the guy, because actually he was possessed by Baby Duval, who in turn is possessed by some goddamn devil from Africa." Schwarz took a quick pull from the beer bottle. "Is that what you're asking me to keep an open mind about?"

Lussac appeared in the French doors behind them, a cigarette dangling from his mouth, another beer bottle dangling from his left hand. His eyes were fixed on a slip of paper torn from a spiral notebook. "How do you boys want to hear it? Sitting down or what?"

Schwarz grinned sardonically. "How about you just give it to us straight?"

The Cajun shrugged. "All right. According to morgue records, she was telling the truth. Louis Dulac, sometimes known as Louie the Horn, was officially pronounced dead on the twentieth of December last year. Cause of death was listed as heart failure. The certificate was duly signed by the Department's own coroner."

"Maybe it was a mistake," Lyons suggested. "Maybe they got the records mixed up with some other poor fool's."

Lussac shook his head. "I don't think so."

"Then what are you trying to say?" Schwarz snapped. "That we've got a real live zombie here?"

Lussac shrugged again, stepped out to the balcony and shut the French doors behind him. "Well, like I told you boys the other day, there could be a scientific explanation."

Lyons frowned. "Tetrodotoxin?"

Lussac nodded, tossed away his cigarette and looked out over the glowing rooftops. "Basically we're talking about a purely physiological reaction. Guy gets hit with that so-called zombie powder and it slows down the vital signs to a point where he *looks* dead. But he isn't. He's just paralyzed. And so when they finally put him into the ground and then dig him up again, he's about ready to believe anything."

"Mind control," Lyons said reflectively.

Lussac smiled. "I guess you could call it that."

"Which brings us back to the Agency," Schwarz added. "Possibly to some sort of CIA psych-op, which pretty well explains everything."

Lussac sighed. "Maybe."

Schwarz looked at him. "What do you mean, maybe?"

The Cajun cocked an eyebrow, then glanced over his shoulder at Carrie, who was seated in the lamplight next to Blancanales. "I just mean that before you start trying to pass everything off in terms of dirty tricks and clever illusions, you might at least listen to what that little lady has to say, if for no other reason than to appreciate the mentality you're up against."

They went back into the hotel room, now filled with the melancholy notes of a tenor saxophone issuing from the radio. A platter of sandwiches and fruit sat on the coffee table, but no one was hungry. Although Carrie had showered and changed into one of the terry-cloth bathrobes furnished by the hotel, it was still pretty obvious that she had been through a hellish ordeal.

Lussac looked at Schwarz and said, "Think of it as indulging the natives. Think of it as ethnological background. But the fact is that if you want to bust Duval, you've got to learn to think like him. And regardless of how many little tricks he employs in order to make his magic work, he's still basically a believer, worse, a *houngan*, a priest of voodoo." Lussac lighted another cigarette and turned to the girl. "Whenever you're ready *chère*," he told her. "They'll listen to you now."

"The spirits are called *loa*," Carrie finally said after an initial hesitation. "Although some are said to have come from the Indians, most originated in Africa, which is where the ancestors also dwell."

"That would be what they now call Benin," Lussac added. "Next to Nigeria."

The girl nodded. "But everyone, the believers, I mean, mostly just think of it as Africa. That's why all consecrated ground is said to be a little piece of Africa, because the spirits won't come down otherwise."

She glanced at Lussac, then looked at the members of Able Team. "There are literally hundreds of *loa* living in waterfalls, streams, trees and swamps. But the primary ones descend from the sky. And to call them down we offer them the things they like to eat and the rhythm of the drums they love to dance to."

She toyed with an empty beer bottle, then tapped the tabletop with her fingernails. "In the beginning the *loa* were the only thing the believers had to keep them in touch with their homeland. Later, when the white masters forced the slaves to convert to Christianity, the old gods still remained. Sometimes the people would refer to them as saints—Saint Michael, Saint John, and so forth—but essentially they were still the old gods from Africa."

"What about Eshu?" Lyons asked. "Is he also an old god from Africa?"

She nodded, then took a deep breath to steady herself. "Eshu is a god of empty spaces, crossroads and time. A lot of people, white people mostly, think of him as Satan, but that's only one of his aspects. In fact, he can be quite helpful as an intermediary between the believers and the greater gods."

"But in the company of Baby Duval," Lussac added, "it's a different matter altogether."

"That's right," Carrie said. "Eshu is very bad in the company of Baby Duval. He's not just a trickster, he's an eater of flesh. He asks for human blood and hearts. He asks to be fed with souls." She brushed a strand of hair from her eyes and shifted her gaze to the darkening sky. Although the moon hadn't quite risen above the peaked roofs, it was obviously going to be another bloodred full moon.

"Tell them about the believers," Lussac said after a short silence. "Tell them how it is among the believers regarding a *houngan* like Baby Duval."

She sighed sadly, then looked at Lyons. "When we talk about the believers, we're talking about a large part of this city. We're talking about thousands of people in all walks of life. We're talking about people who don't just attend the dances on Saturday nights, but people who accept the *loa* with every fiber of their being. We're talking about an entire existence."

She inhaled quietly. "A long time ago when this city was still filled with slaves, the white masters were frightened of the drums and dances, so they tried to put a stop to them. But trying to stop *macumba* is like trying to stop the wind. It just went underground...deep, deep underground. Then, although it was finally accepted again, it never entirely emerged from hiding. But that doesn't mean that it's still not all around us.''

Lyons eyed the young woman. ''So basically you're saying that whatever else might be going on with Duval, whatever links he might have with psych-op specialists, we still have to contend with the people's belief. Is that about the size of it?''

She nodded. ''About two hundred years ago there was a white man named Albert Berry. Now, this Albert Berry made a lot of money in shipping and cotton, but he wasn't satisfied with just being rich. He wanted power above and beyond anything else. So he found himself a *houngan*, who called himself Dr. Hawk. This Dr. Hawk had a special relationship with the darker spirits, the ones like Eshu and the even blacker spirits of the swamp. So Berry said to Dr. Hawk, 'I'll give you all the money you want if you work your voodoo on my behalf so that together we can rule this town.' Well, Dr. Hawk didn't have any use for money, but he did have a use for certain things that money could buy. So he agreed to help Berry, and for seven months and seven days they ruled the world of the believers.''

''So what happened to them?'' Schwarz asked from the opposite corner of the room.

She smiled enigmatically, then shook her head. ''Nobody knows for sure. Some say the dark side simply swallowed them up, the way it's prone to do. Others say that another *mambo*, a powerful voodoo priestess named Sister Clare, finally called down the greater gods to destroy them. Then, of course, there are others who say they're still out in the bayou, waiting to catch the souls of foolish intruders from the north."

"Why don't you tell them what you told me earlier?" Lussac asked.

Carrie shrugged. "It's just a rumor."

"Even so," Lussac replied, "I want you to tell them."

She nodded. "It's about what they say on the streets about Baby Duval."

"And what's that?" Lyons prodded gently.

"They say he's just like that old black sorcerer Dr. Hawk. They say he also has a benefactor, a white man who wants great power through the black blessing of Eshu the Terrible. And even though that white man might not believe in voodoo himself, he knows a lot of people do. Voodoo is his way of controlling them."

"And how do the people suggest we stop him?" Schwarz asked.

She shook her head. "They don't say anything about how to stop him. All they say is that it'll be bad for the believers and maybe even worse for those who don't believe. They say terrible things will happen soon, and it won't matter what anyone believes in the end."

## 9

According to an eighty-nine-page report drawn from Stony Man files and faxed to Schwarz the following morning, Charlie Dawson had originally joined the CIA in the fall of 1958. He had been recruited directly out of Columbia University, where he had received a doctorate in behavioral psychology and a firm grounding in chemical stimulation. Although initially part of the medical staff, he soon found himself working for Dr. Sidney Gottlieb's Technical Services Staff, where, among other things, he helped coordinate the MKULTRA mind control program.

"They called themselves the Sorcerers," Schwarz explained. "There were also the Alchemists and the Medicine Men, but Dawson's group mainly liked to think of themselves as the Sorcerers."

"And these Sorcerers were the bad ones?" Blancanales asked.

Schwarz shrugged. "They were all bad."

Reasonably clear most of the day, the sky was once again clouding over. Schwarz had been up since six in the morning with the fax machine, and now that it was early afternoon he was beginning to feel the effects of little sleep. As for the others, Lyons was bent over the report, trying to puzzle out a traceable lead, while Blancanales paced the floor, hungry and restless.

"In the beginning it was pretty much a defensive action," Schwarz continued as he gulped his fourth coffee on the hotel terrace. "The Agency kept getting reports that the Russians had finally perfected a brainwashing technique, and so it was decided that something had to be done to protect American agents."

"And when was this?" Lyons asked.

"Around 1947. But things really didn't get moving until the early fifties, which is when they started fooling around with LSD, electroshock and a few dozen other nasty things. Then, around 1959, they started getting into even kinkier stuff—low-frequency waves, parapsychological manipulation and what they called ethnological control techniques."

"Which is?" Blancanales asked.

"The study of shamans and witch doctors in so-called primitive societies."

"Charlie Dawson's specialty, right?" Lyons ventured.

Schwarz nodded. "Bingo. What you've got to understand though, is the transition. Although the CIA mind control teams originally tried to figure out how an individual could be brainwashed, they soon started looking at bigger problems—like how to control an entire population. Or how to use local beliefs and superstitions to influence the political process. Now obviously that kind of problem doesn't necessarily apply to the Soviets, but when you start operating in the Third World, then you're into a different ball game altogether. Take Vietnam, for instance. At one point during the Tet offensive, Agency spooks tried to convince the Vietcong that the countryside was swarming with vampires.''

"I remember that," Blancanales said, grinning. "They drained enemy bodies of blood and left them by the side of the road."

"Did it work?" Lyons asked.

"Like a charm," Blancanales said, sighing nostalgically.

"But by the time Charlie Dawson really got going," Schwarz added, "the war was over, and there wasn't any more interest in vampires. So Charlie turned his attention to the Caribbean and started looking into voodoo."

"But basically the goal was still the same?" Lyons asked. "I mean, the whole game was to try to figure out how to win friends and influence people, right?"

Schwarz nodded. "Yeah, I guess you could say that."

"All right, so how do we do the same thing?" Blancanales asked.

Schwarz frowned. "What do you mean?"

"How do we find someone who's not too scared to talk about Baby Duval?"

Schwarz withdrew a slip of paper from the inside pocket of his blazer. "We go in through the back door and have a little chat with a certain local doctor named—" he broke off and glanced at the slip of paper "—Louis Drago Monk."

AT FIVE O'CLOCK that afternoon Lyons, Schwarz and Blancanales finally managed to locate Monk's address. The day had turned quite foul, with rainsqualls and occasional lightning. Although from the outside the doctor's residence looked like any of the refurbished houses facing Algiers Point, from the inside it looked like something out of a low-budget horror movie.

The main ground-floor room at the back was oblong and had four oblong windows facing the gray water of the Mississippi. The furniture looked as if it had been picked up at an institutional auction. A long laboratory table was heaped with papers, stacks of unbound manuscripts and a mountain of books stolen from the public library. Two smaller tables were crowded with bottles and plates of rotting food. Sitting on rows of steel shelves were all sorts of strange artifacts: the bleached bones of alligators and lizards, stuffed cats and birds, beakers of colored liquids, a massive collection of crystallized fossils and what looked like a human brain in a mayonnaise jar.

The doctor, who looked like Hollywood's idea of a mad scientist, was seated at one of the smaller tables when Lyons and Schwarz entered the half-open door without knocking. At first glance he appeared to be part of the pile of junk on the table. Then, very slowly, he rose from the chair and stepped out of the shadows. "I don't see anyone without an appointment," he said. "Besides, the office is closed."

Lyons eased the door shut behind him, while Schwarz began a slow examination of the room. Among the debris deposited on a chest in the corner were two weapons: a sawed-off shotgun and an old Colt revolver.

"We're not here as patients," Lyons said after he made sure the guns were empty.

"Then what?" the doctor asked angrily.

"Let's just say we're students," Lyons replied. "Students of the occult."

The doctor removed a filthy lab coat to reveal an old seersucker suit that was frayed at the edges and stained with what looked like blood. "Who sent you?" he asked over the rims of his Coke-bottle lenses.

"An old friend of yours, you might say," Schwarz said.

"I don't have any old friends."

Lyons examined a glass-encased collection of beetles, some of them the size of a man's hand. "We want you to tell us a story about black magic and a certain little psych-op that was run by Charlie Dawson."

The doctor glared at the two commandos. "You gentlemen don't look like CIA."

Lyons smiled. "Hardly."

Monk shrugged. "I just made some coffee. Care to join me?"

The doctor served strong espresso spiked with brandy, then passed them a humidor filled with Cuban cigars. Schwarz and Lyons exchanged amused glances. Both declined the cigars.

Monk fired up an impossibly long cigar and eyed his guests. "So what can I do for you gentlemen? Or better still, if you're not from the Company, who do you work for? Since you haven't killed me yet, I don't imagine you're hit men."

"Who we work for shouldn't concern you," Lyons said. "But let's just say we know Uncle Sam. As for what we want, I've already told you—Charlie Dawson."

The doctor rose from his chair, walked over to a window and fixed his eyes on the smooth expanse of the river and the slow barges materializing out of the fog. "I never really knew him," he said dreamily. "Charlie, I mean. I worked with him, yes. But in the end I don't think I ever really *knew* him, not in the normal sense." He smiled thinly and puffed on his cigar. "Of course, I don't suppose anybody ever *knew* Dr. Charlie Dawson."

"Spring of '82," Schwarz supplied. "You and Dawson came down here on what they call a loose mandate."

"Very, very loose," Monk said.

"So what was it all about?" Lyons asked.

Monk rested his arm on the cracked sill. "Officially speaking, they called it an ethnological operation. You see, we were under the Technical Services Staff, which at that time was mostly concerned with what I suppose you'd call population persuasion."

"Who was in charge?" Schwarz asked. "Gottlieb?"

"Good Lord, no. Gottlieb didn't even know about it. After all, we were operating entirely beyond the limits of the Agency's charter."

"Who paid the bills?" Lyons said.

Monk turned and peered owlishly at Ironman. "Good question."

Foghorns rumbled from the river now, and sea gulls cried as they circled in the gunmetal sky.

"Now the first thing you gentlemen have to understand is that it actually all started before my involvement," Monk insisted.

"You mean in Haiti?" Schwarz said, recalling the conversation he'd conducted with Crew in Clearwater.

"That's correct," Monk said. "Haiti. Now, of course, at that time Charlie was supposedly somewhat more, how shall I say, in line with regular Agency policies. That is, they sent him down to recruit and place what we generally termed agents of potent influence. And that is precisely what Charlie did, or so I heard."

"So what went wrong?" Schwarz asked.

Monk pressed his palms against the cool pane of glass. "What went wrong?" he echoed. "Baby Shu Duval is what went wrong. Not that Baby was originally an outrageous proposition. After all, Charlie's mandate was to locate and create assets with what you might call popular charisma, assets that could make a difference, politically speaking."

"So where did he come from?" Lyons asked.

"Baby Shu? Where else? From the very bottom of the worst Port-au-Prince gutter. But apparently he had something Charlie was looking for. It was in his eyes, his voice. It was in the sheer bulk of the man. And, of course, Baby Shu had always been a believer."

"A believer in voodoo, you mean." Schwarz said.

Monk let his hands slip from the window. "What else would we be talking about, gentlemen?"

"And what was the Agency's attitude at this point?" Lyons asked.

Monk shook his head in what might have been disgust. "They were delighted, of course. They were tickled pink. After all, Charlie had been ordered to find the sociological handle on Haitians, and he'd found it. Because, you see, voodoo isn't just a superstition down there. It's a way of life. It's the prime force. If you want to control a nation like Haiti, then you'd better learn to deal with *macumba*, which is to say you'd better get yourself a boy like Baby Shu Duval."

"So how did Charlie do it?" Schwarz asked.

"How?" Monk said, pacing the garbage-strewn floor. "In the beginning it was strictly by the book. The boys from psych-ops even drafted a manual on the subject—how to create a demigod in four easy steps. First, of course, you need a subject with that certain kind of look, and believe me, Baby Shu definitely has the look. Next you need a miracle or two to start the ball rolling, preferably something involving a life-and-death issue. In Baby's case I seem to recall that he put a spell on one of the local *houngans*, a particularly odious fellow from one of the outlying villages. And with a little help from one of the Technical Services Staff, the poor bastard died.''

''Who was calling the shots in Langley at that point?'' Lyons asked.

Monk shrugged. ''I'm not sure. Could have been Gottlieb, I suppose. Could have been one of the old Vietnam psych-op directors. The point is, it worked. Within no time at all, word started spreading that Baby Shu Duval was a priest of some consequence, a man to be reckoned with, a voice of the spirits.''

''And what was the political angle?'' Schwarz asked.

''Nothing special. It was simply felt that if the Agency could establish Baby Shu as a potent force in the area, they could use him to short-circuit any Communist guerrillas.''

''Really?'' Lyons said skeptically. ''How so? By casting spells on them?''

Monk nodded. ''Exactly. After all, who'd want to follow the Commies once it was established that the spirits didn't like them? They tell me it worked quite well in Nigeria and the Congo.''

''Then what was the point of bringing it all to New Orleans?'' Schwarz asked.

''Ah,'' Monk said, ''the sixty-four-thousand dollar question. That's why you're here right now, isn't it?'' He crossed the room to where an old map of the city was tacked on the wall. ''I suppose in one sense Charlie just wanted to see if it could be done. He wanted to see if he could create his own little kingdom in an American city. Then, too, he needed money, which meant he needed a ready market for his contraband.''

"Coke?" Lyons prompted.

"And harder stuff. You see, by the time Charlie transplanted his operation to the French Quarter, he was no longer really working for the Agency. In fact, I guess you'd say he wasn't working for anything but his own mad vision. And, by the way, he is mad. That's the first thing you have to understand."

Lyons leaned forward and rested his elbows on his knees. "How did it happen?"

"Well, I suppose in one sense you might say he succumbed to the worst of all occupational hazards associated with psychological operations—he started to believe in his own tricks. He started to believe that Baby Shu really was a demigod, which in turn made Charlie believe himself to be a god. Then, too, of course, voodoo can be very seductive. The drums, the chanting, the dancing, all very seductive. And so, although Charlie continued to rely on various tricks of the trade, he no longer believed they were just tricks. He'd listen to those drums and those frenzied voices and they'd echo deep inside him and convince him that he was all-powerful."

"Who worked the tricks?" Lyons asked.

"Charlie had this specialist who used to work in Hollywood. Very good at makeup and things like that."

"Does he have a name?"

Monk searched his memory for a moment. "He called himself Mexico, I think. Roger Mexico. Funny name, eh? No doubt false."

"What about the chemical side of things?" Schwarz asked.

A bemused look spread across Monk's ravaged face. "You mean the zombie powder, I take it?"

Schwarz nodded.

Monk moved from the map to the rusting steel shelves. He picked up a jar of yellowish powder and slowly turned it over in his hands. "Now you must understand that I didn't actually invent the process. I just refined it, isolated the active ingredient, as it were."

"Tetrodotoxin?" Schwarz ventured.

"Exactly. Although, in all honesty, I must confess the drug alone isn't the key. The key is the psychological manipulation of the victim's belief system after ingestion. You see, once the victim has been paralyzed, it's important to instill the belief that his soul has been removed, that he's actually dead and thus entirely under the control of his master. Now, of course, there are any number of variables, and more often than not the process is only partially effective. But that's basically how Charlie Dawson creates his zombies."

"And where does Dawson get his victims?" Lyons asked.

Monk shrugged. "Various places. Some, of course, are shipped in from Haiti. Others are picked up from the general riffraff one finds in the New Orleans slums.''

''And how many are there?'' Schwarz asked.

''Difficult to say. Twenty, thirty, possibly forty. But the point is, that once it became known that a zombie *could* be created, that it was, indeed, a reality, then all sorts of local believers began flocking to Baby's cause.''

Lyons stood and went over to one of the windows. ''So what was your role in all this?''

Monk dropped into a chair and sagged. ''I guess you might say I was the technical adviser.''

''Regarding the tetrodotoxin?'' Lyons asked, sitting down again.

''Yes. But you have to understand that when I was directly involved it wasn't entirely out-of-bounds. I mean, there was still a connection with the Agency.''

''What part of the Agency?''

''Technical Services, of course.''

''And what was their game?''

''Well, they wanted the process, naturally. They wanted to make zombies.''

''What for?''

''What do you think? Control. They wanted complete control of the human will. I mean, just think of the possibilities. One could actually create an entire platoon of zombies who have no concept of fear, men who would do anything no matter what the consequences. Besides, Technical Services is always looking for more effective methods of psychological control. That's their job.''

"So when was the last time you saw Charlie Dawson?" Schwarz asked.

"I don't know. Six, maybe eight months ago."

"Where?"

"Here. He came to collect some things."

"What sort of things?" Lyons pressed.

Monk took a deep breath, then shook his head. "He wanted the tetrodotoxin formula."

"And you gave it to him?" Schwarz asked incredulously.

Monk sighed. "What else was I going to do? He had one of his zombies with him. They're very effective persuaders. Anyway, I've been waiting for someone like you two to show up. Someone I could tell everything to."

"Why didn't you get in touch with the police?" Schwarz asked.

"Take a guess."

"And you're not afraid now?" Lyons asked.

"I've never been more afraid in my life. But now it's done. Finally."

Lyons and Schwarz got up out of their chairs and headed for the door. As they moved through the doorway, Monk suddenly called out, "By the way, it's not all chemical."

Lyons turned and looked at him. He had fired up another cigar. "What are you talking about?"

"The tetrodotoxin is pure science, but there are other factors. Call it magic if you like. Call it uncharted psychological transference, but there's definitely more to Baby's power than just powder and tricks. I'd walk softly if I were you.''

Out in the street it was unseasonably cold, and the fog had grown quite thick again.

"Well?'' Blancanales asked, as Lyons and Schwarz slid into their rented Oldsmobile.

"Well, nothing,'' Schwarz muttered. "This whole goddamn city is wigged out.''

"Yeah, but did he tell you anything useful?'' Blancanales persisted.

Lyons shrugged. "Hard to say.''

Blancanales inserted the key into the ignition, but didn't turn it.

"Incidentally,'' Lyons said as he scanned the street ahead. "You didn't happen to see anything unusual, did you?''

Blancanales shook his head. "Nothing to write home about.''

"Nobody hanging around while we were in the house?''

Blancanales shook his head again, this time with a frustrated sigh. "Nobody worth mentioning.''

"What do you mean, nobody worth mentioning?''

"Just a couple of drunks.''

"What kind of drunks?''

"I don't know. Drunk drunks. They went down that alley next to Monk's house.''

Schwarz leaned forward from the backseat. "Hey, Carl, what's gotten into you?''

Lyons shook his head and shifted his gaze to the entrance of Monk's house. "I don't know. Just a feeling, I guess."

"Yeah, well, maybe you should take that feeling and—" But Gadgets was interrupted by the first scream.

As Lyons and Schwarz leaped from the car, they heard a second and third scream. By the time they reached the steps, though, it was suddenly very quiet.

Lyons drew his Colt Python, pressed himself against the doorway, and motioned Schwarz to do the same.

"You smell what I smell?" Schwarz whispered, holding his nose.

"Yeah," Lyons replied. "Rotten meat."

"Or zombies," Schwarz cracked.

Lyons snapped off the safety on his gun and braced himself. The front door was ajar, offering a glimpse of broken glass, scattered papers and a shattered dish in the first room. But it wasn't until Lyons moved cautiously into the laboratory at the back of the house that he got a good look at what voodoo was capable of. A human heart lay on one of the tables in full view.

**10**

"Maybe you'd better just stay where you are," Lyons told Gadgets.

But Schwarz shook his head and stared from the doorway. "Too late," he whispered.

At first glance there seemed to be only a minimal amount of blood—a small stain between the doctor's legs, another beneath his head, and still more that had trickled out of his mouth. Then, by degrees, Lyons noticed that there was actually blood still seeping from the heart on the table. And there were more splashes of blood in the narrow hall leading to the kitchen, off to one side of the laboratory.

"I suppose you realize they might still be in the house," Lyons whispered to Gadgets. "Do you understand what I'm saying?" he snapped when Schwarz didn't respond. "I think they're still around here somewhere."

"How can you be sure?" Schwarz finally asked.

"Because I can fucking feel them!"

Lyons followed the trail of blood into the kitchen, where it continued up a service staircase to the second floor. On the first step he found chicken feathers. On the third step he found the doctor's left hand.

"I want at least one of them alive," Lyons growled. "I don't care what you do to the others, but I want at least one of the bastards alive."

"Maybe they took off down the front staircase," Schwarz whispered. He looked at the kitchen door. "Or maybe they're in the backyard."

At the top of the service stairs they discovered bloody footprints.

"Looks like there's three of them," Schwarz ventured. "Two in rubber shoes, the third one barefoot."

Lyons scowled. "I don't care if there's twenty of them. I still want one of them alive."

They paused at the top of the stairs and peered around the corner. The blood trail seemed to vanish.

"They're toying with us," Schwarz whispered. "They know we're in here. They want us to be."

Lyons didn't listen, though. His eyes were fixed on the dim outline of something scrawled on the wall ahead. A grinning face in blood? There was also a small heap of what looked like spaghetti, but was undoubtedly another part of the doctor's anatomy.

"See what I mean?" Schwarz said. "They're toying with us."

Someone had smashed the lights, leaving the second floor very dark. The stench of rotten flesh was particularly bad now, and shadows flickered everywhere.

"No matter what happens," Lyons whispered, "just remember that they're human beings. They'll fall down like anyone else."

"Sure," Schwarz rapped, looking at the coil of intestines on the floor. "Human."

By now the shadows had coalesced into a single inhuman form, something with an enormous head and impossibly long arms. Schwarz jumped as the thing sprang out of the darkness and engulfed him. He fired as he fell to the linoleum, squeezing off two blind rounds from his Colt Python. He tried to fire again as a damp hand encircled his throat and another clamped his wrist. Above his head he saw a glint of steel and looked into smoldering, deep-set eyes. Then, before he could even gasp, Lyons's .357 Magnum boomed three times.

"It's a goddamn mask," Lyons whispered.

Schwarz rose to his knees, picked up a bloody fragment of papier-mâché and turned it over in his hands. Although two 158-grain hollowpoints had pierced the right eye and shattered the snout, the basic form was still discernible: a vaguely smiling alligator head, the kind of thing one saw everywhere during Mardi Gras. "Yeah," Schwarz rasped. "A mask."

The body lay sprawled against the far wall—a heavy black man in a cheap plastic raincoat and running shoes. Although the left eye was still fixed in pain and horror, the right side of the face had been literally blown away. There was also a deep wound in the throat.

"See what I mean?" Lyons crowed as he kicked the lifeless head. "They fall down and die like anyone else."

"Sure," Schwarz said, looking around furtively at the flickering shadows.

They moved down the hallway slowly, pausing to kick doors open and check rooms. When they got to the main staircase to the ground floor, they hesitated and peered down into the gloom.

"Let's take this slow and easy," Lyons said.

"No argument out of me," Schwarz muttered.

"Remember," Lyons whispered, "we've got to take at least one of them alive."

When they reached the bottom of the stairs, Schwarz checking behind to make sure no one sneaked up on them, they were greeted by what looked like a swaying cobra and a gorilla or bear. Other shadows suggested a prancing spider or giant crab.

But in the end it was the fairly ordinary shadow of a man that nearly took Lyons's head off with an eighteen-inch knife.

Ironman spun, the soles of his shoes skidding on the blood-slick floor. He heard the blade descending with a low hiss, then a gutteral grunt as the shadow lunged at him from a dark recess. The blond commando fired two quick shots at the giant's gut. Then, spinning again to avoid the blade, he squeezed off a third shot, hitting the man's chest.

Without thinking, Schwarz fired three rapid blasts that literally split the killer's skull, sending blood and tissue to oblivion.

*Cult War*

"Next time go for the knees," Lyons whispered. "I'm trying to save one of these bastards, remember?"

Schwarz shrugged. "Easier said than done."

"Yeah, well, I still want a live one. They don't wear bulletproof vests on their knees."

They found a side door to the house open and carefully worked their way out into the alley. At the end of the passageway was a garden wall and the river.

"Maybe he jumped the wall," Schwarz suggested, scanning the vine-encrusted bricks. "Or maybe he took off down the river embankment."

"No," Lyons breathed. "He's still down there... waiting for us."

They moved down the alley in a half crouch, keeping an eye on the rooftops. When they reached the low wall, they each took turns looking over it. There were a few palms, magnolias and a couple of cypress trees, but no zombies.

"How do you want to play it?" Schwarz asked, watching the deeper shadows near the cypresses. "Do you want to split up and try to catch him in a squeeze, or do you want to just flush him out?"

Lyons shifted his gaze from the cypresses to the placid river. He heard the squeal of a slow-swinging gate, followed by the sound of slow footsteps somewhere behind the house. "Let's try to flush him out in the open."

"What if he won't go for it? What if he tries to bolt?"

"He won't, but you stay back here just in case."

There was a small pond choked with lily pads and rotting branches near the cypresses. There was also an empty bird cage dangling from one of the trees. Closer to the far edge of the pond, Lyons found footprints in the matted grass and a human ear.

He stopped, unable to take his eyes off the bloody lump of flesh at his feet. Although he glimpsed something from the corner of his eye, something like a dark claw snaking out from below the pond's surface, he couldn't tear his eyes from the severed ear.

Until he actually felt it...actually felt the cold hand locking on his ankle like a vise and dragging him into the pond.

Lyons should have guessed. The guy had been hiding underwater, probably breathing through a hollow reed. He hit the water headfirst and felt the slime invading his mouth. As the shock of the attack registered on him, he also felt his Colt Python slip out of his fingers.

The zombie tried to bite through his throat as if he were an alligator and Lyons an unfortunate deer. The Stony Man commando twisted the creature's arms and caught a quick glimpse of its disfigured face. He struck out at the thing's jaw, then felt a massive fist slam into his chest, winding him. But as his chest began to burn and panic threatened, he was suddenly conscious of something else—blind rage.

He lashed out at the killer's eyes first, digging for the soft membrane and raking with his nails. Then, pushing away from the big black man, he kneed him in the groin and karate-chopped his throat. The assassin bellowed and lost his grip around Lyons's neck, allowing Ironman to twist away and launch a vicious kick at the zombie's groin again.

Air.

He got free of the slimy water and heard the creature moan behind him. Turning, he wrapped an arm around the bastard's throat, and squeezed.

The struggle seemed eternal as the black man writhed frantically at the edge of the putrid pond and Lyons squeezed with all his might. Then, very suddenly, it was over, and the black man stiffened.

"I think you crushed his goddamn windpipe," Schwarz commented behind him.

"Where the hell were you?" Lyons gasped.

"You seemed to be doing okay by yourself. Besides, you didn't want me to blow any more of them away."

"This one's still alive," Lyons growled. "You can bet on it."

They dragged the huge man away from the pond, and Lyons began to pump his chest. When the killer started showing more obvious signs of life, Lyons pulled out a pair of plastic handcuffs and secured his wrists. Then, for a long time, he just looked at the man's heaving chest, his defiant eyes, the smear of theatrical makeup across his cheeks and forehead.

"Doesn't look too scary to me," Schwarz said. "In fact, he doesn't look too bad at all."

"I still wouldn't let my daughter marry one," said Blancanales over Schwarz's shoulder.

"Maybe one of you guys should call Lussac," Lyons said coldly. "Tell him to bring a couple of uniforms and to prepare one of the interrogation rooms ... someplace isolated and preferably soundproof."

"I already did," Blancanales said. "What about his rights? Don't you think we'd better read him his damn rights?"

Lyons turned and glared at Blancanales. "What rights, Pol? Zombies are dead, aren't they?"

## 11

"Maybe he doesn't speak English," Schwarz said.

"Or maybe Carl was right," Blancanales suggested with a smile. "Maybe the bastard really is a zombie."

It was eight-thirty in the evening. Lussac had initially arranged for an interrogation cell in the relatively empty east block, but Lyons still hadn't been satisfied, so they transferred the man to one of the older basement cells.

The cell was essentially just a gray-green concrete box, bare except for a naked light bulb and a bolted chair. There was, however, a rectangular sheet of one-way glass set into the wall opposite the prisoner's chair, a voice-activated recording system and speakers behind the wire mesh. Thus, while Blancanales and Schwarz watched and listened from behind the glass, Lyons and Lussac conducted the interrogation.

They began with simple questions: name, address, place of birth and employment. Finally, in a fit of rage, Lyons grabbed the man by the collar of his filthy jacket and slammed his head against the wall. In response, the prisoner just stared into nothingness, totally devoid of emotion.

"How about you let me have a try?" Lussac asked softly. "After all, we certainly have nothing to lose, do we?"

Lyons glanced past the lanky Cajun's shoulder, meeting the prisoner's blank gaze. "All right, you try talking to him."

The cell was roughly fifteen-by-eighteen feet, but it took Lussac at least six or seven seconds to cross the concrete floor and position himself in front of the handcuffed prisoner. Then, for another three or four slow seconds, he simply looked at the man, vaguely smiling with a hand on his hip and a cigarette dangling from his lips.

"Now the first thing I want to tell you," Lussac began, "is that I do, in fact, happen to know what you're thinking. That is, I might be just a poor little Cajun boy who don't know nothing about voodoo and such, but I do indeed know what you're thinking. You're thinking that if you open your mouth, even for a moment, ol' Baby Shu Duval is going to get you. Now ain't that right? You're afraid that if you even so much as tell us your name, ol' Baby Shu is going to slip under that door or ease himself through the cracks in the wall and steal away your immortal soul? Ain't that right? Ain't that precisely what you're thinking this very moment?"

Although the prisoner didn't really respond, there was a momentary flicker of understanding in his eyes.

"That's what I thought," Lussac continued. "You see, maybe you don't believe everything Baby tells you. In fact, maybe you even think he's a little full of shit occasionally. But just to be on the safe side, you don't want to take chances. You don't want to take the chance that he really can steal your soul and stick it in a clay jar."

There seemed to be another brief flicker of understanding in the prisoner's eyes, a moment when the man almost seemed on the verge of speaking. But then it passed and he stiffened into stony silence.

"All right," Lussac continued in an easy drawl. "Let's try another tack, shall we? Let's say that if you start telling me about Mr. Baby Shu, I'll personally guarantee that your immortal soul remains intact. Now, you say, how can a white boy like myself make a promise like that? Well, I'll tell you. It just so happens I have some pretty powerful *gris-gris* of my own. It might not be exactly the same brand of *gris-gris* Baby Duval has, but it's powerful. It's real powerful. In fact, I'd venture to say that with a little luck I might be able to mix up a spell or two that even Baby Shu can't match. Now what do you say to that?"

Once again there was something in the prisoner's eyes, some fleeting indication that Lussac was getting through.

"And you know I'm not just spitting in the wind, don't you?" Lussac continued. "You know I'm just another poor white Cajun boy, but by the same token you also know that I do indeed have certain prime connections to the spirit world, connections that just might be as powerful as anything Baby Shu Duval has got going for himself. And if I were to, let's say, invoke those connections, to call down those spirits, so to speak ... well, I think you know what I'm talking about now, don't you?'' Lussac smiled and briefly locked onto the prisoner's eyes. ''Yeah,'' he rasped. ''You definitely know what I'm talking about.''

''Nicely played,'' Lyons said to Lussac when they joined Schwarz and Blancanales in the corridor outside the cell. ''Very nicely played.''

''Only problem is,'' Blancanales said after pouring a cup of rank coffee, ''what are you going to do for an encore?''

Lussac grinned, accepted the coffee from Blancanales and planted another cigarette between his lips. ''What do you think I'm going to do? I'm going to do exactly what I told him I'd do. I'm going to call in my personal voodoo connections and make that old boy sing like a bird.''

''And exactly how do you plan to do that?'' Schwarz asked.

''Why, with a telephone. How else?''

BUT CARRIE LATROBE DIDN'T own a telephone, nor did her neighbor Jolly Trumain, nor his neighbor Louise Gilbert. However, there was a telephone in the Blue Note Café where Carrie sometimes sang on Friday and Saturday nights, and there were any number of local residents who were more than willing to deliver a message.

It was almost midnight when Carrie arrived at the police station with an escort of two uniformed cops. There was no introduction, greeting or preliminary explanation. From the moment she appeared on the staircase, it was obvious she knew precisely what Lussac wanted.

"Once I start," she told the Cajun police inspector, "there will be no turning back. You understand that, don't you?"

Lussac nodded. "No one's going to change their mind, *chère*."

"I also need to be alone with him," she added. "You've got to free him from the chair and leave me with him."

Lussac glanced at Lyons, who returned the look with an expression that said, *Can we have a word?* The two men then withdrew down the corridor where Lyons whispered, "What the hell do you think you're doing?"

Lussac smiled, then glanced over his shoulder at Carrie. "Well, you know what they say, ol' boy. Sometimes in order to catch the fox you have to act like a chicken."

Lyons shook his head with a frown. "The man in that cell isn't kidding, Renny."

"Of course he's not kidding, *cher*."

"Then why did you bring the girl down?"

Lussac tapped his forehead with an index finger. "Because up here, in his head, that ol' boy in there genuinely believes Baby Duval will torch his soul if he talks to us."

"And you think Carrie can convince him otherwise?"

"I do."

"And what happens if he goes crazy?"

"Then we move in fast, no?"

Lyons looked at Carrie, letting his eyes linger on her exquisite profile for a moment, then sighed. "All right. We'll play it your way."

She entered the cell slowly, moving to the far corner and keeping her eyes on the gray concrete until Lussac had freed the prisoner's hands. Then, carefully, she let her eyes meet the prisoner's cold stare. Outside, Lyons, Schwarz and Blancanales remained at the one-way glass like Peeping Toms. When Lussac joined them, gently shutting the cell door behind him, he said, "Well, I told you we did things a little differently down here, didn't I?"

Carrie knelt on the floor to unpack her leather satchel. From where Lyons and the others stood, she might have been unpacking a picnic basket, laying out the cold cuts, mustard and soft drinks. Except that there was an obvious intensity to her movements, a sense of raw power that electrified the cell. And she had begun to sing softly, sweetly, whispering syllables that spoke of a truly remote and primitive place, a place of scorched horizons and red mud, a place where locust storms blotted out the sun and thunder continually echoed among the blasted rocks.

Although the prisoner stayed in the chair, his vision locked onto the opposite wall, his face suddenly became a mask of perspiration, and he trembled from head to toe.

"Think of it as reverse psychology," Lussac whispered to the members of Able Team. "Duval has convinced that poor bastard that his immortal soul is in danger. So we're turning it around for him.''

"Yeah, but what exactly is she doing?" Blancanales asked.

"Exactly?" Lussac smiled. "She's calling to the spirits. She's trying to get their attention."

"And what's in the bowl?" Lyons asked, noting a plastic bowl of pale brown liquid.

"Whiskey," Lussac explained. "Whiskey for the gods."

"And the cigars?" Schwarz asked, noting that the girl had placed four cigars on a chipped porcelain dish.

"Same thing," Lussac replied. "But depending upon one's school of thought, the offerings are only symbolic. What matters is the faith, the faith and the need."

Carrie slipped off her sandals, stood and began gently swaying back and forth. On the other side of the one-way glass it looked like a casual dance, a few unthinking steps to some half-heard song on the radio. But there was an unearthly intensity to her movements, a sense of ancient power snaking up through the soles of her feet and pounding through her veins. Her hands seemed to move independently of her arms, her legs independently of her hips, her head independently of her shoulders.

"You sure she's all right?" Lyons whispered.

Lussac nodded. "She's letting the spirits inhabit her body," he replied. "She's drawing them in with her breath and letting them take control."

"What happens if they don't want to let go?" Schwarz asked.

Lussac frowned. "Then she's in trouble."

The dance stopped as suddenly as it had begun. One minute Carrie was swaying with frantic intensity, the next she was absolutely motionless, her left hand extended above her head, her right hand in front of her face, her gingham dress swept back to reveal a naked thigh.

When she finally spoke, the words tumbled out mechanically from deep within her body, and the harsh, grating voice couldn't have been more alien. "Who are you?"

The prisoner shuddered and clenched his fists.

Carrie repeated the question, her voice growing drier, harsher. "Who are you?"

The prisoner's head jerked, and he met Carrie's gaze. "Nobody," he snarled. "Nobody."

"Then where are you?" she asked softly. "If you are nobody, where are you?"

"In da dark. I be in da dark."

"And who is with you in the dark?"

"Eshu. Eshu of dull spaces."

Carrie looked intently at him. "Eshu of dull spaces."

"What's happening now?" Lyons asked, his face pressed against the one-way glass, his right hand fingering his Colt Python.

"Call it spiritual rapport," Lussac replied. "She's managed to contact his spirit self by means of her own spirit."

"Is that dangerous?"

"Not necessarily."

"But what did he mean when he said he was no-body?" Schwarz asked.

"I think he's trying to tell her that his soul isn't in his body, that his soul was captured by Baby Duval and banished to the realm of Eshu."

"Is that bad?" Blancanales asked.

Lussac nodded. "Yeah, that's bad."

Carrie began to sing again. Although most of the words were unintelligible, Lyons and the others caught something about a pile of bones slowly turning white beneath a juniper tree, and something else about a man with no shadows. She also sang about a waterless landscape, a pack of sleeping dogs and sullen faces gazing from baked mud huts. In response, the prisoner just stared at Carrie, his head cocked at an awkward angle while his eyes remained glued to hers.

She hesitated, her dance becoming an underwater dance, her arms moving like shifting seaweed. Then, gradually shifting her gaze to look at the prisoner, she asked, "And where is Mr. Baby Shu?"

The prisoner shivered, then moaned, "Everywhere. Baby be everywhere."

"Then let me see him," she coaxed. "Let me see him."

The prisoner leered. "See him? But you already be seeing him."

"Maybe we should do something," Lyons whispered to Lussac. "Maybe this thing has gone far enough."

The Cajun shook his head. "It's all right. It's still just dialogue. They're just talking through their respective mediums."

"Yeah, but the bastard seems to think he's Duval."

"So?"

"So aren't we starting to play it pretty close to the edge?"

"That depends."

"Upon what?" Schwarz asked.

"On just how much power Baby Shu really has."

Five minutes passed, five entirely motionless minutes during which the prisoner continued to stare into Carrie's eyes. Then, slipping into a trance, the leer faded from his lips.

Carrie approached slowly, her fingers white with chalk, her dress swept back to reveal dark, slender thighs. She extended a cautious hand, slipped to her knees and gently traced a cross on the prisoner's forehead. "For the *loa* of light," she whispered. "For the *loa* of light and sky."

The prisoner shivered slightly and he seemed to have difficulty breathing. "For the *loa* of light, eat shit," he smirked. "For the *loa* of light, eat shit and die!"

Carrie started singing again, her voice as soft as the murmuring wind or the slow beat of a dove's wing. "For the *loa* of light, I say, begone. I say, begone, and leave this soul to me."

The prisoner clenched his teeth, and traces of blood formed on his lips. Carrie continued singing to him, tracing another white cross on his wrist and whispering into his ear. "For the *loa* of light, I say, begone. Be banished to the rocks and water. For the *loa* of light, I say, be banished to the sky, the grass and the sand. For the *loa* of light, I say, begone, and leave this poor soul alone."

All the while, the prisoner writhed and spit out a litany of his own. "For the *loa* of light, eat shit and die. For the *loa* of light, eat shit and get yourself back to the sky."

"He's fighting her," Lussac said. "That's what the chanting's all about. He's trying to keep her from kicking him out."

"What are you talking about?" Lyons asked, his right hand still fingering his weapon nervously.

"Duval. He's trying to resist being banished."

"You mean to say that man in there thinks his body's possessed by Duval's spirit?" Schwarz asked.

Lussac nodded. "Although, if you feel more comfortable with a psychological framework, you might want to call it a transfer of personalities. At some point the prisoner became so psychologically overwhelmed that he actually took on Duval's personality."

"Then what's to keep him from attacking her physically?" Blancanales asked.

"The spirit that possesses her," Lussac replied. "The spirit of white light inside her will protect her."

The dialogue had grown softer, little more than a chorus of dry whispers as Carrie kept asking, "Where? Where? Where is your home, Mr. Baby Duval?"

To which the prisoner continued to respond, "Eat shit and die." But the question was clearly sapping the man's strength, leaving him limp, staring, barely able to move even his head.

"Where? Where?"

Then, suddenly lunging from the chair and knocking Carrie aside, he burst into a bone-chilling scream. "Dablaakhool! Looookmeeupindaablakhoolbitch!"

Lyons drew his Python and moved to the door. Before he could turn the lock, though, Lussac grabbed his arm. "Not yet. Let her play it out."

Lyons looked at him. "What do you mean, play it out?"

"It's too late to stop it now. She's got to see this through. She's got to meet him head-on."

"He's right," Schwarz said. "Step in now and we could lose both of them."

The prisoner moved back and forth across the cell, crying "Blaaaakhoooool! Looookmeupindablaakhoolbitch!"

But Carrie kept hammering away, asking, "Where? Where? Where?"

Finally there was only silence again, a dead, frozen silence that seemed ageless. Carrie knelt and whispered, "Where? Where is Baby Duval?"

The prisoner shook his head.

"Where?"

The big black man hunched his shoulders and gritted his teeth. Then, suddenly throwing his head back, he howled, "Blaaaakhoool! Blaaaakhoool!"

"Where?" she prodded. "Where?"

"Blaaaaaaaaaaaaaakhoooooooooool!!" the prisoner shrieked one last time.

Lyons was four feet from the door when the killer made his move. He vaguely heard someone, maybe Blancanales, shout, "Grab his legs!" He also thought he heard Carrie scream something like, *"Macumba! Macumba!"* But by the time Ironman dashed into the cell, the prisoner was diving through the air.

A moment before he hit the wall, the zombie stiffened in order to intensify the impact. The sound, faintly audible above the screams, sounded like a melon bursting on hot concrete.

"Is he dead?" Schwarz asked softly.

Lyons placed a finger on the prisoner's throat, probed for a pulse, then shook his head. "Yeah, he's dead."

Lussac appeared, gently lifted Carrie to her feet and led her out of the cell. "It's not your fault, *chère*," he whispered.

Carrie didn't seem to hear, though. She just gazed dully in front of her.

"So what do we do now?" Blancanales asked.

But no one answered him.

Carrie was sent home, the body was removed and a patrolman named Tyler was dispatched for coffee and doughnuts. Lussac, Lyons and the others then moved upstairs to one of the second-floor briefing rooms, where Lussac pecked out a report on an ancient typewriter. Meanwhile, Blancanales sat on a chair and guzzled coffee, while Schwarz, seated at a desk, busied himself with a recording of the interrogation. He listened and relistened to the voices through the earphones attached to a cassette player. Lyons, for his part, just stared out the window and watched the rain fall.

"Anybody know how to spell schizophrenia?" Lussac asked finally.

"Yeah," Blancanales said sullenly. "V-O-O-D-O-O."

A young inspector named Albert Lee appeared and whispered something about liability insurance in Lussac's ear. The Cajun smiled and said, "Don't worry, Al. Something tells me nobody's going to sue us over this one."

Finally, following another long silence broken only by the clatter of the typewriter and the tap of rain against the glass, Schwarz announced he had found something.

"Now I don't pretend to know a whole lot about psychology," Schwarz began, "but I do know this—whatever made that guy bash his head into the wall had to be one mean force. Call it transference. Call it voodoo. The fact is, that guy was under some kind of heavy psychological pressure to keep his mouth shut. So, when Miss Latrobe put him in a position where he believed he had no choice but to speak, he killed himself."

"Get to the point," Lyons said wearily.

"The point is, if you take away all the mumbo jumbo, it kind of makes sense. First the guy is told that if he betrays Duval, the evil spirits will seize his soul. Then he's told that if he doesn't tell the truth, the good spirits will grab his soul. Well, naturally he's got no choice but to bash his head against a wall.''

"Yeah, but that still doesn't tell us anything,'' Blancanales said. "What's the point?''

"The point is, that guy wasn't just screaming his head off in the end. He was trying to tell us something. He was trying to respond to Miss Latrobe's interrogation. She kept asking him where we could find Baby Duval, and he actually tried to tell her.''

"Except that he took a swan dive into the concrete before he could get it out,'' Lussac said.

"Not necessarily,'' Schwarz replied, switching on the cassette player.

At first the words were entirely unintelligible. "Blaaaakhooooool! Blaaaakhooooool!'' In the background they heard whispering: "Where? Where?''

"Now listen to this,'' Schwarz said as he adjusted the switches and toyed with the volume.

"Blaaakhooool! Blaaak Hooool!''

"Black Hoool?'' Blancanales repeated. "What the hell's Black Hoool?''

"Nothing,'' Lussac said. "Black Hoool is zip. But Black Hollow is a little place about thirty miles from here. It's an old Indian burial ground on the edge of the swamp.

"And that's what you think he was trying to say?'' Lyons asked.

Lussac shrugged and moved to a map of the city on a bulletin board. "Black Hollow is right about here, six miles beyond the highway along one of those little roads that washes out every spring and fall. Now and again we hear talk about draining the swamp and building a golf course, but nothing ever happens."

"Anybody living out there?" Lyons asked.

"A few Indians and some hermits who spend their days poaching off public lands and running moonshine."

Lyons picked up a ballpoint pen, moved to the map and indicated a one-inch grid near the Lake Pontchartrain Causeway. "What about this area?" he asked. "What's it called?"

Lussac smiled. "Funny you should ask."

"How so?"

"Well, according to my mama, that particular portion of the hollow happens to be called Zombie's Cove. It's not a name you'll find on any map, but that's what they call it."

"Anyone live out there?" Schwarz asked.

Lussac shrugged. "Well, now, I reckon we'd better find out."

## 12

In no time at all, using the police computer, Schwarz dug up the name of someone in the Black Hollow area who might serve as a lead to the whereabouts of Baby Duval. His name was Raymond Anderson.

"So who is he?" Lyons asked Gadgets.

"Good question," Schwarz replied. "Originally he moved into the neighborhood about sixteen months ago. Previous address was Langley, Virginia. Before that, however, he lived out in Hollywood where he worked as a free-lance makeup and special effects artist under the name of Roger Mexico. Sound familiar? His last known credit was a low-budget horror flick called *Sex Vampires of Mars*."

Lussac appeared in the doorway of the briefing room. Behind him, with a box of doughnuts, was Blancanales.

"Did you came up with Anderson's current occupation?" Lussac asked.

"Special effects consultant," Schwarz replied.

"How about an address?" Blancanales asked.

Schwarz nodded. "Right on the edge of Zombie's Cove."

ZOMBIE'S COVE WAS a lonely place where giant tiger lilies bloomed and luminous green logs lurked like drowned corpses beneath the murky water. Dense fogs were frequent, and the afternoon Renny Lussac and Able Team headed out to the cove one was already building up.

Raymond Anderson's house stood on a willow rise above the cove. It was an old structure, probably built at the turn of the century by a long since bankrupt planter. Anderson himself was a small, intense man with little hair and pinched features. He smiled quizzically when he opened the door to Lussac's knock. Upon catching sight of Lussac's badge, however, his smile quickly faded. "I hope you gentlemen have a warrant," he yelped as Lussac and Able Team barged into the foyer. "Because if you don't—"

"Shut the fuck up," Lyons said. He turned to Schwarz and Blancanales. "Check the bedrooms." Then he pushed Anderson into a shadowy parlor and tossed him onto the sofa like a rag doll.

"So, Anderson, Mexico, whatever your name is," Lussac said as he examined the contents of a cabinet, "where is he?"

Anderson, wearing a gray bathrobe and a mismatched pair of slippers, looked forlorn. Then he heard the sound of breaking glass from the kitchen and winced.

"Where's who?"

Lyons picked up a sheaf of envelopes sitting on a bureau and flipped through them, stopping at

"P.O. Box 921, Langley, Virginia. Langley. Now that's a familiar place."

"Where's your employer?" Lussac demanded, ransacking a bookcase as he searched for letters that might be concealed between pages.

"My employer?" Anderson bleated.

Lussac whirled around and grabbed the little man by the collar of his bathrobe. "Charlie Dawson, Anderson. Where the hell is Charlie Dawson?"

Anderson swallowed hard, then jumped when he heard pine splintering upstairs. "Look, I don't know what you're talking about. I'm just here on a film shoot."

"Yeah?" Lyons said from the end of the room where he was searching a desk. "And what film would that be? *Night of the Voodoo Zombies*?"

Suddenly there was a chorus of activity from the staircase that led to the basement—sounds of bursting locks and cracking plaster. Then over the din of the search, Blancanales shouted, "Hey, maybe you guys better come down and take a look at this!"

In contrast to the living quarters the basement was relatively clean and well lighted. Shelves lined the walls and an aluminum table sat beneath fluorescent lights. There was also a drafting table, soldering boards and stainless-steel washtubs. What immediately caught the eye upon entering the room, though, were the faces of zombies, at least fifteen "death masks" molded in polyurethane and mounted along the far wall. Also scattered here and there were rubber torsos and plastic arms and legs.

"So, Mr. Hollywood," Lussac said as he pushed Anderson into the room, "what's all this about?"

Blancanales picked up one of the plastic legs, and examined the fake wound on it. "Pretty realistic."

"Like I said," Anderson muttered. "I'm in the film business. I do special effects."

Lussac examined the contents of a packing crate marked Dawson Imports. Among the wads of shredded newspaper were all sorts of electrical components, including three or four voice-activated microphones, a miniature switching device and four bulletproof vests. Then, without warning, he drew his gun and pointed it at Anderson. "All right, creep, this is how we're going to play it. You're going to start giving me nice, clean answers. You're going to start cooperating or we're going to make those zombie masks of yours look pretty compared to what your face will look like when we get finished with it."

"I want to speak to my attorney," Anderson tittered on the verge of hysteria.

"There are no lawyers in hell," Politician snapped. "And that's where you are now."

"So, Anderson, how about it?" Lussac growled. "What's the deal here? You been helping Charlie with his horror show or what?"

Anderson shook his head, then sagged to the floor. "Look, it's just a job. Charlie saw my work out in Hollywood and asked if I'd like to try my hand at something different."

"How long ago was that?" Lyons asked.

"About eighteen months ago."

"And what was the arrangement?" Lussac asked.

Anderson shrugged. "Nothing special. Charlie just wanted me to work out a few special effects for the project."

"What project?" Lyons demanded.

"He called it psych-ops. He said he wanted to prove it could be done."

"Prove what could be done?" Schwarz pressed.

"That he could create a voodoo god in a modern American city. Naturally Charlie is insane. That's the first thing you've got to understand. But that doesn't mean he's not a genius."

"Yeah, we know all about Charlie's intelligence," Lussac said. "Where does the coke fit in?"

Anderson smirked. "Where do you think? After all, a scam like this isn't cheap. I mean, apart from the staff, you've also got to pay guys like me, and I don't come cheap. Besides, Charlie may be crazy, but he's not stupid."

"Meaning?" Lussac replied.

"Meaning he's not about to turn down an opportunity to tap into a sixty-million-dollar pipeline, not when there are a lot of hungry mouths to feed."

"Hungry mouths?" Lyons questioned.

Anderson smiled crookedly. "Well, let's face it, Charlie might not be operating with the CIA's blessing, but he still has a few guys in Langley who support him."

Lyons and Lussac exchanged wary glances, and Schwarz immediately began a search for microphones. In the end, however, all he found was another collection of rubber feet with amazingly realistic sores.

"Tell us about Baby Shu," Lyons said at last.

Anderson smiled. "You familiar with *Franken-stein*? I mean, the book, not the movie. Well, that's Baby Shu. The guy is so incredibly fucked up he even believes his own tricks. Of course, it isn't all tricks. There is a certain psychological angle to this voodoo stuff. He's out there in some kind of satanic Never-Never Land."

"Which you helped create," Lyons said grimly.

Anderson grinned awkwardly. "Hey, it's what I do for a living. It's Hollywood. You want to make a guy look like he's been rotting in the grave, I'm your man. You want to make a guy look like he's Superman, I'll fix him up with a vest. I also do a little sound effects work, make it seem like there are voices coming at you from out of the walls. But I didn't have anything to do with guys getting cut up. I had nothing to do with that shit at all."

"Who killed Antoine Dunn?" Lussac asked.

"I don't know. Maybe a guy named Jacques, or another guy called Monroe."

"And where would we find these characters?" Lussac asked, stepping closer to Anderson, his eyes almost homicidal.

Anderson gulped. "Look, I got no objection to testifying or anything like that, but you got to get me out of here. He'll kill me."

"Where can we find Dawson and Duval?" Lussac growled.

Anderson wilted. "There's this place."

"What place?" Lussac snapped.

"It's out along Great River Road near a little stretch of bayou that Charlie calls the Gorge. There's an old mansion out there called the Burnside House. That's where most of the heavy stuff goes down."

"What about those so-called zombies?" Lyons asked.

"They're out there, too, mostly living in slave cottages or in one of the basement chambers. But you've got to understand that they're not just a bunch of hypnotized goons. They're shock troops, well trained and extremely well armed. And a lot of them have had experience fighting in the Haitian drug wars, so they're not exactly new to this game."

"How many of them are there?" Blancanales asked.

"More than you can handle. Maybe more than anyone can handle."

They radioed a squad car to pick up Anderson, waited until it showed up, then headed back to the city in Lussac's Cutlass. The return trip was subdued and quiet. Finally, after leaving the Lake Pontchartrain Causeway, Lussac pulled the car onto the shoulder and shut off the engine. He eyed the others in the rearview mirror. "Look, maybe we should talk."

"Sure," Lyons said, "let's talk."

"The way I see it," Blancanales piped up, "this is just another job. These guys may have been given that tetrodotoxin stuff to make them think they're immortal, but in the end there's no mystery here. There's no magic. There's no walking dead. There's just us, them and a full metal jacket.''

"I don't think anyone's going to argue with you, Pol," Lyons said. "Isn't that right, Renny?"

Lussac smiled. "No comment."

**13**

At approximately the same time that Pol Blancanales was dispelling the voodoo myth, Carrie Latrobe was wrestling with questions of reality. It wasn't the first time she'd entertained doubts about the unseen world. Even as a child there had been a part of her that refused to accept the *loa*, a part of her that said, "There may be a God in heaven, but there are no spirits in the bayou." Uncle John had told her that doubts were natural. He'd told her that all great mediums suffered a crisis of faith periodically. But Carrie didn't just question her faith. There were simply times when she didn't want to believe.

She lay on her bed, watching the overhead fan revolve slowly, and thought about spiritual possession, deciding that it was altogether possible that there were no spirits. Perhaps it really was all just psychology, mind control. She thought about the notion of death by spells and told herself that it was possible that a victim died solely because he believed he would die. Finally she thought about zombies, deciding it was all just a matter of chemistry.

In opposition to this kind of thinking, however, there was another part of her that couldn't help but believe, a part of her that saw the spider inching across the blistered wall. *An omen.*

Another part of her watched the torn curtains swell with the breeze.

*Baby Shu is near.*

Suddenly the air became oppressively warm. And then she heard footsteps.

She propped herself on her elbows and peered through the half-open door at the vague outline of something or someone passing through the foyer. Slipping off the bed, she glanced instinctively around the room for a weapon—a knife, a pair of scissors, anything. Briefly she considered a prayer to Oxum, a quiet prayer to invoke his strength, but finally she just fell to her knees and waited.

The zombies entered slowly, hesitating for a moment in the doorway, then pausing again when they finally spotted her. The first one was tall and slender with what looked like an open wound in his throat. The second was short and stocky with what looked like a blind left eye. They wore ragged tuxedos, top hats, filthy spats and fingerless gloves. The taller one carried a rusty butcher's knife. The short one hefted a blackjack and had a burlap sack slung over his shoulder.

She didn't scream. She simply waited until they reached the center of the room, then bolted for the open window. When the short one attempted to grab her ankle, she managed to fight him off with a swift kick to the groin. But then the tall one grabbed her by the hair, wrist and throat.

She was only half conscious when they slipped the burlap sack over her head, bound her hands behind her and carried her out to their old sedan. She was only vaguely aware of the sunlight through the sack, the cool breeze on her bare legs, and then finally the darkness as they stuffed her into the trunk. At one point she distinctly heard them laugh above the rattle of the tires on the gravel.

For a while, lulled by the sound of the tires on the highway, she almost slipped into another dream, a dream in which all the holy spirits waited in the forest to save her. But by the time she felt the pavement give way to dirt and the stench of dust fill her nostrils, all she could think about was Duval . . . Baby Shu Duval.

Although she was still blindfolded when they led her into the house, certain impressions were unmistakable. She was fairly certain, for example, that the house was old, probably one of the antebellum estates that were rumored to be haunted. Next she was also aware of the smell—scented candles mingling with the stench of death. Finally she was also aware of the presence of pure evil.

She initially saw nothing when they removed the burlap sack. Nothing beyond a dark shape among the darker shapes of furniture. Then, gradually, the faint outline of a man became discernible, an enormously fat man with sleek features and piggish eyes. He wore a vaguely luminous sharkskin suit with a gold watch chain across his ample belly. His front teeth were also gold, and there were at least three diamonds on the fingers of his left hand. But what really made her tremble was his voice. It was the soft, melodious voice of the fiend she had always known was waiting for her.

"Hello, Carrie, my dear, how are you today?"

She shut her eyes as he drew closer, wrinkling her nose when she got a whiff of his cheap cologne.

"Do you know who I am, my dear?" he asked politely, gently brushing a strand of hair from her face.

She nodded, but still kept her eyes shut.

"Then say it, my dear. Say my name."

She shivered again and attempted to turn her face away as he gently took hold of her chin.

"Come on, my dear. Say it. Say my name."

She felt her lips soundlessly form the first syllable, felt the name virtually explode in her brain.

"That's right," he breathed. "Say it."

Tears streamed down her cheeks. "You're Baby Duval. Baby Shu Duval."

He smiled, revealing yet more gold teeth and a moist, pink tongue. "Yes, I am Baby Shu Duval and I am everything you dreamed about, everything you imagined and more."

He stepped to one side so that he could examine her face in the flickering light. Although she had opened her eyes again, she kept her gaze fixed on the far wall, where a thin white man with gray hair and eyes watched.

"Now, of course, the question is, what do we do with you?" Duval said. "For example, do we shoot you? Burn you? Feed you to the gators?"

She heard him chuckle, then shivered again as he traced a finger along her slender throat.

"Or do we…make you our bride?" He ran a finger along her spine, then slowly traced the outline of her right breast. "Now tell the truth, my dear, hasn't the thought ever crossed your mind? Haven't you ever wondered what it would be like to let your power mingle with mine?"

She felt his lips touch her ear, felt his hot breath on her neck.

"Think about it for a moment. Think of all the power we could hold if we were only to merge, to bring the dark and light together in a glorious union of passion."

She opened her eyes again and caught another blurry glimpse of the silent white man seated in the corner. Then, feeling Duval's fingers slide across her breast, she quickly squeezed her eyes shut again.

"And, oh, how the spirits would rejoice," Duval whispered as his lips drew closer to her mouth, as his noxious breath filled her nostrils. "Oh, how they would sing and dance when I hold your body close to mine. And it would be a very beautiful thing. A very, very beautiful thing."

But before he could actually kiss her, the white man finally rose from the chair and stepped forward. "That's enough," he said. "That's quite enough."

Carrie was removed to the basement, and Duval turned to the white man. "You don't know what you're dealing with. She's no ordinary woman."

Charles Dawson grinned. "Not now, Baby. Not now."

In addition to bourbon on the sideboard, there was also a bottle of fifteen-year-old Scotch. Pouring himself a large one, Dawson stepped to the window. From there he had a good view of moss-draped oaks, bent cypresses and soft willows. Although there were moments, usually in the evenings, when these surroundings tended to inspire all kinds of supernatural instincts, usually Dawson remained unmoved. He believed in chemistry and psychology, but he didn't believe in his creation—Baby Shu Duval.

The chimes of the grandfather clock upstairs sounded, then the lesser chimes of a wall clock in the parlor. It was five o'clock in the afternoon.

"I must make that call now," Dawson said.

Duval sat on the flowered divan and reached for the bourbon. He would have preferred something with a little more kick, such as a rail or two of Bolivian White, but he knew Dawson wouldn't approve. Drugs were a commodity, Dawson was fond of saying, never an indulgence.

"These people of yours," Duval said at last. "Who are they?"

Dawson sighed wearily. "Haven't we been through all this before, Baby?"

Duval shrugged. "Hey, I just want to know who they are, okay?"

"Associates. They're associates of mine."

"From headquarters?"

"That's right, from headquarters."

"White folks from headquarters?"

"Yes."

"Then what do we need them for? Why the hell do we need these white folks from headquarters when we've got all my children?"

Dawson slowly traced a circle in the dust along the windowsill. "We need them because we're no longer dealing with a bunch of frightened cops. We're dealing with professionals, and your children, as you call them, aren't professionals."

"So what are you going to do? You going to bring in these professional white men from headquarters to shoot these other professional white men?"

"If need be, yes."

"Well, my children can do their own shooting. My children aren't afraid of no white men. My children are only afraid of me!"

There were voices from the corridor below, then the sound of fiddles on the radio. Returning to the window, Dawson caught a glimpse of a muscular black man swaying in the shadows beneath the oaks. Although he had never been able to remember all the names of Duval's followers, he seemed to recall that the man below was called Sleepy.

"And what about the girl?" Duval asked.

"What about her?"

"When am I going to have her? When am I going to make her my little blushing bride?"

Dawson shook his head, then took another sip of Scotch. "You'll have her when I'm ready to give her to you and not a moment before. Now, if you'll excuse me, I have to make that telephone call.''

There was only one room in the sprawling house that Dawson considered his own. An oddly shaped room, almost octagonal with a rank of oval windows affording a view of the swamp, it was situated along the southern corridor at the top of a narrow staircase. Children might have once played there, for the wallpaper still bore the faded imprint of cowboys and Indians.

Dawson had chosen the room for his office because it was remote and commanded a broad view of the grounds below. On a somewhat less logical level, however, he liked the room because of its ambience, because of the quiet sense of magic it seemed to invoke. Not that Charles Dawson necessarily believed in magic. But having spent the better part of twenty years exploiting the superstitions of others, a little superstition was bound to rub off.

On this particular Thursday afternoon, however, his thoughts were strictly on down-to-earth matters. He had always known that sooner or later there would be trouble from the local police, but he had never anticipated difficulties from a group like the one Renny Lussac had acquired.

In response to the threat from Lussac's free-lance commandos, whoever they were, Dawson had contacted two former CIA associates. The first, a one-time operative in Southeast Asia, had told him there was little or nothing he could do to help. Even when Dawson attempted to remind the man that a good portion of his cocaine profits had gone to support the Agency's covert effort, the man turned him down.

The second man Dawson telephoned was more helpful. A seasoned veteran of the Central American wars named James Potter, he agreed to help Dawson . . . for a price. "It's mainly just a question of pulling together the proper resources," Potter had said.

"And how long will that take?" Dawson had asked.

"Give me till Thursday."

In all, Dawson had to place three telephone calls before he was able to reach Potter a second time. Finally, after a long wait, Potter came on the line. "So what's happening?"

In the background Dawson heard the clink of glasses and silverware, a woman's laughter and the Beatles' "Nowhere Man."

"It's about what we discussed the other day," Dawson said. "My little problem with free-lancers."

"Yeah, well, it so happens I might have a solution for you," Potter said. "Only problem is that it's going to cost."

"How much?"

"Fifty grand for me and ten each for my boys."

Dawson frowned and stared at the faded cowboys and Indians on the wall. "Look, it's not like I haven't got people down here. I've got at least thirty guys who—"

"You've got punks," Potter cut in. "Brainwashed, drugged-out punks. Now they might get lucky, but then again they might not. And believe me, I think

I've got a line on the boys you're dealing with. They've got some kind of connection with Justice, and if I'm right, they're the best in the business.''

Dawson sighed. ''All right, I'll get you the money, but I'm going to need you down here tonight. I think these guys are ready to make their move.''

''You think?'' Potter snapped.

''Well, we've had some indication that—''

''Let me tell you something, Charlie, you're not playing trick or treat anymore. You're playing hardball, which means you better not just think. You better know. Now is there any way you can find out exactly what their plans and intentions are?''

Dawson bit his lip and thought of Carrie Latrobe in the basement. ''Yes, I think so. I mean, yes, I do.''

''Then I suggest you get moving. Because when me and my boys arrive, we'll need to know precisely where everything stands. Understand, Charlie?''

''Sure,'' Dawson said. ''I understand perfectly.''

But for a long time after replacing the receiver, Dawson remained at the window, desperately trying to make sense of everything, trying to puzzle out what was happening to him. In the beginning it had all seemed so simple: the establishment of a voodoo lord among the believers in New Orleans. All it had really depended upon was timing and creation of the right illusions. Although he had never necessarily approved of using his operation for the distribution of cocaine, he had always been a realist—and money was a necessary reality. He had also known that certain people would probably get hurt. But from the occasional intimidation of a few local troublemakers to the wholesale slaughter of a government enforcement team was a big step. Things definitely seemed to be getting out of control.

In all, Dawson must have spent at least an hour reviewing his early operational notes, leafing through dozens of scribbled pages in an effort to determine what had gone wrong. Just recently he'd begun to think of himself as a kind of Dr. Frankenstein—a basically well-intentioned man who had somehow created a monster, who in turn created monsters. Not that he had ever had any doubts about what kind of person Baby Shu Duval was. But by the same token, who would have ever imagined the man would actually start to believe in his own illusions?

UNKNOWN TO DAWSON, though, Baby Shu didn't believe in his illusions completely. Yes, he had to admit there were moments when the magic seemed pretty damn real, and that people's minds seemed capable of causing all sorts of strange phenomena. Still, he never forgot that his power was scientifically based, which didn't necessarily diminish it.

When Dawson had moved upstairs to use the telephone, Duval had returned to the parlor and poured himself another tall bourbon. He often sat there in the late afternoon surrounded by the symbols of his power: a mummified cat, a jar of chicken blood, two or three satchels of herbs and an AK-47 that Dawson had brought down from the north.

He also enjoyed the view from this room, the long, dreamy view that led to the supposedly haunted swamps. On this particular afternoon, however, his thoughts were mainly focused on the room below, the basement room where Carrie Latrobe now resided.

Although Duval had finally come to realize that there was nothing in heaven and earth that couldn't be explained scientifically, he had to admit there was definitely something special about Carrie. It was in her eyes, in the way she moved, the way she talked. He couldn't put his finger on it exactly, but there was definitely some sort of power in the girl.

And he wanted that power for himself.

"We'll never achieve absolute dominion over the riffraff in this city until we come to terms with her," Dawson had told him. "Too many people listen to her."

"So what do we do?" Duval had asked.

"We must either destroy her or bring her into our fold."

To that end, Dawson had devised all sorts of clever tricks. He had embedded directional microphones in the walls of her house. He had unleashed a box of garden spiders beneath the pantry door. He had even sent her a drugged and hypnotized zombie with an uncanny ability to imitate Duval's voice and mannerisms. Yet it wasn't until Duval had seen her photograph that he had personally started to take an interest in the girl.

He had thought about her a lot in the days and weeks preceding her kidnapping. He'd imagined her seated on his knee in this very room, listening to him talk about his power. He'd dreamed of her reclining on his bed, waiting for him to emerge from his bath. He'd fantasized her response to his every need, indulging his every whim. And he'd visualized her in every imaginable pose... except death.

"It's time," Dawson said from the doorway suddenly. "It's time to deal with our guest."

Duval put down his bourbon and turned to face the white man. In the evening shadows Dawson couldn't have looked more menacing. Behind him stood one of the more unfeeling members of the operation—a lean and clearly disturbed killer from Martinique named Monroe.

"Let's go," Dawson said. "It's time."

Duval rose from the chair, then frowned. "We aren't going to hurt her, are we?"

Dawson shrugged. "We're going to do what we have to do. Now let's go."

"Yeah, but what about my marriage?"

"It's become a tactical matter. We've got to find out what she knows."

"But you said I could have her. You said I could—"

"Now, Baby," Dawson commanded. "Now."

CARRIE LAY on the filthy mattress with her knees drawn up to her breasts and her face half buried in her arms. Although earlier she had been unable to stop herself from crying, her eyes were dry now.

Her cell was little more than a bare box with two dusty windows that were barred and probably led nowhere.

For a long time after they threw her into the room, she considered all sorts of terrible possibilities. She thought about the policeman who had had his heart cut out and the thief who had thrown himself out of the window. She also thought about the monster she had killed near the river and the prisoner who had bashed his head against the wall. But most of all she thought about what it must have been like to be turned into a zombie, to die and yet remain fully conscious, to live and yet remain entirely under the control of someone else.

Then, by degrees, she gradually regained some shred of hope. If Duval wanted her dead, he would have killed her a long time ago. She thought about Renny Lussac and realized it wouldn't be long before someone informed him that she was missing. Finally she also thought about Renny Lussac's friends, particularly the tall blond one named Lyons.

She was still thinking about Lyons when the bolt slid back and Baby Duval entered the room. He was accompanied by the gaunt white man and a particularly savage-looking black man. Although the black man carried a knife, her eyes remained riveted on something in the white man's hand—a needle and syringe.

"Don't be afraid," Dawson whispered as he drew a little closer. "Zombies live forever."

# 14

It was just after six in the evening. After receiving a telephone call from Osmond Massard regarding a disturbance at Carrie Latrobe's home, Lyons and the others had met Lussac at the station. When they entered the briefing room, they found the conference table littered with black-and-white glossies. There were photographs of Carrie's parlor, the floor littered with broken glass and upended furniture; of the door that had obviously been kicked in; and three or four shots of footprints and tire tracks.

Initially Lyons's reaction was purely practical. "Who made the call?"

"Some old guy named Uncle John," Lussac replied.

"But nobody actually saw anything?"

"No," Lussac said. "No one."

Then, after glancing through the photographs and gazing out the window for a few minutes, Lyons suddenly declared that the girl was alive. It wasn't a logical deduction; it was just something he sensed in every fiber of his body.

Massard reappeared, wearing a blue nylon windbreaker and a baseball cap. Behind him stood two similarly dressed officers from the SWAT team. "Just spoke to the chief. He's going to let us go, but on a strictly volunteer basis."

"What about the State Police?" Lussac asked.

"State is out. In fact, State doesn't even want to know about it."

"So how many does that leave us?"

Massard sighed. "Twelve, fifteen, something like that."

"That should be enough," Schwarz said from the end of the conference table.

Massard frowned. "Maybe."

"What do you mean?" Lussac asked.

"He means," Blancanales said, "that Dawson and Duval might bring in some outside talent."

"Who told you that, Pol?" Lyons asked.

"It just figures," Blancanales replied. "Dawson's former CIA and still has a lot of friends."

"Any idea what kind of talent?"

Blancanales shrugged. "Your guess is as good as mine. But you know how nasty their boys can be. Especially the rogue ones."

"Well, just the same," Lussac said, "we have to go for it."

"There's no question about that," Lyons said. "It's just a question of when."

FOR REASONS OF SECURITY they assembled in the basement briefing room. In all, thirteen New Orleans police officers had volunteered to storm Burnside House. Most were in their mid-twenties. Three were from the narcotics squad, two from vice and the rest simply patrolmen. En route from the third floor, Lussac had explained that the majority of those who had volunteered were either blacks or Cajuns, and thus, to some extent, their motives were culturally based. When Lyons confronted the men, however, he saw only the faces of soldiers.

The meeting began with a short introduction as Massard rattled off the men's names. Then there was a brief word concerning procedure and jurisdiction.

"Now most of you have probably heard a whole lot of ugly rumors," Lussac said. "Stories about what happened to Dunn and other people around town. But I just want to tell you that what we're facing are your common garden-variety drug dealers and murderers. Suspected drug dealers and murderers, I might add. There aren't any real zombies or voodoo priests out there. There's just a few suspects, period."

A thin fair-haired officer named Danny Paris raised his hand. "Exactly how many suspects are we talking about?"

Massard responded first. "Could be as many as thirty or forty, but we don't anticipate all of them resisting."

"And what are they armed with?" a stocky black man named Crosby asked.

"M-16s. Maybe some AK-47s," Lyons replied tersely.

Another black man stepped forward, a lanky fast-talking narcotics officer named Cal Davis. "Now, ah, let me get this straight. Thirteen of us and you guys are about to move out against some ol' spooky swamp house in order to take thirty or forty freaked-out zombies armed with assault rifles and God knows what else? That about the size of it, sir?"

Lussac grinned. "Well, I wouldn't exactly describe it quite like that, Cal, but now that you mention it, yeah, that's about the size of it."

Davis nodded, then stepped back into line with the others. "I just thought I'd ask, that's all."

In closing there were also a few words about tactics. Basically, Lyons said, they would be playing it by the book. The men would be divided into assault and backup teams. Those in the assault team would be under his direction, while Massard would command the backup. They'd move out in two vans, but would do the last stretch on foot. Although there was no reason to believe the grounds of Burnside House had been rigged with electronic sensors, anything was possible given the kind of resources at Dawson's disposal. It was also remotely possible that Dawson's people might be armed with submachine guns. So, in order to even the score, he and his friends had brought a few special weapons of their own. Ironman then turned to Blancanales, who held up an SMG.

"This, gentlemen, is the H&K MP-15," Lyons said. "I'm sure you SWAT people are familiar with this baby. She accepts a fifteen- or thirty-round magazine and squeezes out those rounds at eight hundred per minute. She also features a delayed blowback selective fire and doesn't weigh much more than your service revolvers." He turned to Blancanales again and was given a hand-sized metal object. "For a little more punch, we're also going to issue you with a few of these M-19 fragmentation grenades."

Next, turning to Schwarz, Lyons was handed a strange-looking rifle. "And for you men in the backup team, I have this little darling—the IDG M-36 sniper system. You'll find that it closely resembles and feels like the M-14, but has been converted to reduce its overall length. It features an integral flash blind and a muzzle brake to reduce the blast by about eighty percent. It won't help you much for the final assault, but it should allow you to pick off a target from up to three thousand feet. It's also user friendly for those without long-range experience. Now, are there any questions?"

"Yeah," Davis said, "I got a question. Just who are you guys, anyway?"

As Baby's face drew closer, it seemed to fill the whole room.

That was Carrie's first thought: the man's face was like one of those comical balloons sold in Jackson Square that just kept getting bigger and bigger. There was also something strange about his eyes. They could have been plugs of volcanic glass or black pearls. But strangest of all was his voice, which seemed to reverberate off the walls.

"Now what you crying about?" he whispered.

She shook her head and watched his elastic face expand more while his glassy eyes became darker.

"Because you don't have no need to cry," he murmured. "You don't have no need to cry at all. Because even though you may soon be dead, I'll still have the power to revive you with a kiss. I'll still have that power even though you may be dead for all the world to see. Now ain't that something? Ain't that just something fine?"

She shook her head again, and said, "Please. Please." Then, catching another glimpse of the white man's syringe, she began to sob.

But Duval only smiled. "Now listen to me, girl. It's just like the man says. You got nothing to fear but fear itself. Because even after you're dead, I'll still be with you. I'll still be talking to you, singing to you, letting you know how much I love you. And even if you can't move your little finger, you'll still be hearing me. You'll still be hearing me and thinking about me and knowing that you're going to be my queen."

She caught a glimpse of the white man nodding to the tall black man, then felt her shoulders being pinned to the floor. She saw Baby's face withdrawing again with an oddly tender grin as the white man's face drew closer. She heard one of them say, "Hold her steady." While another, probably Duval, whispered, "It ain't nothing." Then she felt the prick on her arm, and her own voice crying, "No!"

She felt as if she were falling.

That was her second thought: slowly falling into a gray void. At the same time she also felt the cold spreading like a pool of black ice from the pit of her stomach to her limbs. She shut her eyes with a wave of dry nausea and heard a distant voice say, "That should do it." She was vaguely aware of Baby's hand sliding across her forehead while the white man lifted her wrist to feel her fading pulse. "Yes," he said, "that should just about do it."

She felt her heart slow, her breathing fade to almost nothing. Then, although she still heard voices, they seemed to make no sense.

"Youheeermedarling?" Baby whispered. "Youheeerme?"

While the white man murmured, "Giffher amooooment to reeeajuice."

Next she felt herself floating, drifting into a deeper blackness that smelled of sulfur and more cigars. She was also vaguely conscious that there were others around her, at least two dozen half-crazed faces watching from the flickering shadows. Then, although she could no longer actually see Duval, no longer actually hear him, she couldn't have been more aware of his presence, of his lips very close to her ears, his voice filling her head as he spoke.

"That's right, darling, I'm with you. I'm right here with you, inside your heart, inside your brain, inside your very soul."

He may have kissed her. She didn't actually feel it, but somehow she knew he had. And she was pretty certain his left hand had begun to caress her breast while his right hand brushed the hair from her forehead. Meanwhile, the white man continued to check her pulse, peer into her eyes and press his fingers against her throat.

But the body, Baby told her, was merely an illusion. The body wasn't real. All that was real was the soul, and her soul was now his. "And that's how I'm speaking to you now, little darling," Duval murmured. "I'm talking to your soul. I'm talking directly to your very soul. And your soul is mine. *Mine!*"

There were distant echoes of other voices. But they seemed to come from inside her head, as in a dream, rather than from the corners of the room.

*"Gris-gris. Gris-gris. Macumba."*

She sensed another presence drawing closer, a dark, hungry fiend in top hat and tails. She sensed the icy chill of his gaze, the dark flash of his grin and finally his voice like tiny needles in her brain.

"Welcome to the zone of Eshu," he said. "Welcome to the land of intersections."

She sensed him drawing closer still, then felt him literally merge with Duval to become a truly awesome power. But the voice was still soft, internal, hypnotic.

"You're dead now," he said. "You're dead to everyone but me, and I'm dead to everyone but you."

She felt him reach inside her again, enter through her nostril and touch the core of her being. She also felt his icy presence in her brain again, whispering over and over, "You are mine. Mine. Mine."

*So this is what it's like to be dead,* she thought. *This is what it's like to be possessed.*

Baby-Eshu whispered in reply, "That's right, honey. You're possessed, completely possessed."

But at the same time she sensed a second presence—very distant but quite strong. It seemed to come from beyond the walls, from deep among the cypress boughs where the mist gathered in undulating pools. She sensed it calling to her, reaching out across a mile of shivering leaves to embrace her with a strong arm.

*Carl, is that you?*

*Yeah,* Lyons told her, *It's me. Hold on.*

Dawson put down the needle and turned to a wiry mulatto named Dickerson. "What do you mean, they're here?"

"I mean that Scooter seen 'em," the mulatto replied. "He seen 'em."

"Where?"

"Just beyond where that ol' road forks. Then he saw 'em again down by the stream."

"How many?"

"Ten, maybe more."

Dawson pursed his lips and gazed blankly at the wavering shadows around him, at the girl still prone on the floor, at Duval still hunched above in his ill-fitting top hat, at the dozen or more half-crazed believers still seated against the far wall, rocking in time with their chants.

So much for elaborate illusions, he thought. So much for tricks.

He turned back to Dickerson. "Go find the others. Tell them to get their weapons and position themselves around the grounds."

Dickerson nodded thoughtfully. "I'll tell 'em. I tell 'em just like you told me. But I know what they're going to say. They're going to ask about da *gris-gris*. They're going to ask why Baby ain't out there stopping them with his magic and his *gris-gris*."

Dawson bit his lower lip in an effort to control his mounting rage. "Tell them the *gris-gris* is in their rifles."

## 15

Blancanales placed a hand on Lyons's shoulder. "Are you all right?"

Lyons turned to look at his friend. "Yeah, I'm all right."

They were lying beneath curtains of Spanish moss and a canopy of spidery ferns. Although the mist was quite thick on the forest floor, there was still a clear view of the red clay road between ranks of tiger lilies.

"She's still alive," Lyons whispered as he stared straight ahead. "She's still alive."

Blancanales reached for the big man's arm again. "What did you say, man?"

Lyons shook his head. "I said let's move out."

Two trails lead from the clearing where the assault team had left their vans. The first, winding through thickets of willows and swamp grass, roughly paralleled the old road. The second, skirting the edge of the marsh, wound through a mango grove and led directly to Burnside House. Lyons chose the first path because it was darker and less traveled.

Lussac appeared, slipping out from behind a cluster of vines. "Danny Paris thinks they might have spotted us."

Lyons digested this possibility for a moment, then looked at the path again. "It doesn't matter whether they've spotted us or not. We're still going ahead with it."

They moved out in single file: Lyons on point, followed by Lussac, Blancanales, Schwarz, Davis and Paris. Although there were distant cries of birds and what might have been a snoring gator, the forest floor was mainly cloaked in silence...and the burgeoning mist.

"Kind of reminds you of Nam, don't it?" Schwarz whispered to Blancanales as they crept along the sodden path. "Sort of like the Central Highlands."

"Yeah," Blancanales whispered, shivering.

But as they moved in closer, and could see the house, it became quite clear that they were in a place unlike any other. This wasn't Vietnam, Central America or Africa; it was more like a suburb of hell.

They had stopped in a stand of willows where the ground was soft and stank of rotting leaves. With the fog and the encroaching darkness, the landscape around them seemed smudged, ethereal, unreal. The green-gray shades of moss mingled with the dark blue shadows of twilight and merged with the sky.

Danny Paris appeared, followed by Cal Davis. Both men carried SMGs. "They're definitely close," Paris said.

"Where?" Lyons asked.

"Just beyond that stretch of marsh," Davis replied.

"Armed with?" Lussac asked.

Paris shook his head. "Can't tell. Maybe AKs, or Uzis."

"But I'll tell you one thing," Davis added.

"Yeah, what's that?" Lyons asked.

"Judging by the way they move, these guys aren't a bunch of crazed animals. They've played this game before, and like it."

They moved out again at a somewhat slower pace, keeping to the deeper shadows among the palm-shaped forms. Waterbugs swung on intricate trapezes, fist-sized fungi flowered on rotting logs, and enormous butterflies and moths banged against their heads. But what really caught their attention was the cottonmouth.

"Just out of curiosity," Blancanales whispered to Lussac, "how deadly are those things?"

Lussac glanced at the four-foot, whiplike snake. "I don't reckon they're any worse than what you encountered in Nam."

Blancanales looked at Schwarz, then back at the snake. "That's what I thought."

There were pools of dark water beyond the cypress trees, filled with rotting logs where more cottonmouths lay waiting for an ankle or hand. There were also small clouds of mosquitoes, hornets and horseflies. But what finally brought Lyons and Lussac up short was a very different kind of threat: the double click of an assault rifle.

Lyons dropped into a low crouch and scanned the dark foliage ahead. "Tell me something about them," he rasped.

"Like what?" replied Lussac.

"Like anything. Anything that'll help me understand them."

Lussac wet his lips, shook his head, then said, "All right, the first thing you've got to remember is that it's old, real old. Older than Jesus, older than Judaism, older even than Egypt. It comes from the source of all civilization, the cradle of all human existence. I mean, you get these anthropologists, right? And they dig up these old bones of people who were more ape than man. Well, it probably all began when the first ape looked up at the sky and began to wonder who he was and where he came from."

There were hints of movement among the far oaks, shadows playing on shadows, forms emerging from formlessness.

"Where does Baby Shu fit in?" Lyons asked.

"Like I told you before, Baby Shu's the link. He's what you might call the physical incarnation of the dark side. Now maybe five or ten thousand years ago ol' Eshu was just another spirit from the void. But these days he's bad. These days he's the unholy trinity—the incestuous father, the hag mother and the foul ghost. He's what you might call the nightmare of nightmares, and he does everything in reverse."

A distinctly human shape briefly appeared between vine-roped sweet gums, and there were sounds of something moving through shallow water.

"But however you choose to see it," Lussac continued, "you've got to bear in mind that these people are determined. They're tapping into something mighty powerful, something white boys like you and me can't even begin to understand."

Now there was a dark figure crouched among the willows that ringed the edge of the marsh, and that was something Lyons definitely understood. He lifted a fist in the air to signal the others, then burrowed into the rancid leaves.

THE THIN MAN IN THE WILLOWS lowered his weapon and scanned the mist-shrouded marsh. Known to the others as Louis LeCloud, he was one of the oldest members of Baby Shu's following. To his left crouched yet another brother from Port-au-Prince named Charlie Durange, and past Charlie were two local boys known as the Florabel twins. All in all, their frame of mind was precisely as Lussac had described it—determined.

There were also cottonmouths among these willows, but Baby had told them that the serpent was their friend. So, too, were the mosquitoes, toads and bats. "Because when you are one with Eshu," Duval had said, "all his creatures be your friends, all his creatures lend their eyes and ears to help you eat my enemies. You just got to have faith. You just got to have faith in my power, which is also the power of Eshu the Black Smiler."

And Louis LeCloud definitely had faith in the power. He had faith in the mosquitoes that tormented

Lyons's neck and wrists, faith in the salamander that slithered past Schwarz's ankle, faith in the toad that watched Lussac and faith in the crow that kept an eye on Cal Davis.

But most of all he had faith in the serpent that inched down from the sweet gum vine to within a foot of Danny Paris.

PARIS SCREAMED before he realized the snake was harmless. He screamed with a sudden vision of those terrible eyes, that uncoiling body and the fangs in his thigh. He screamed as he fell, tripping over lily roots and sinking to his knees in swirling water. Yet when the first slugs tore into his chest, tossing him back into the vines, he didn't even whimper.

Davis responded first, sliding through the rotting undergrowth to cradle the wounded man in his arms. "Just be still, brother," he whispered. "Just be cool and lie still."

But Paris had already begun to convulse, spitting up bubbles of blood from his lungs with a horrible shiver. "This is bad," he coughed. "Real bad."

There were more shots from the willows, and four slugs cut through the foliage above Blancanales.

"We've got contact!" someone shouted. "We've got fucking contact!"

Schwarz responded next, spraying eight 9mm rounds into the darkness. Then, slithering forward through a tangle of sodden vegetation, he squeezed off the remaining slugs in his magazine.

"You see anything?" Lyons yelled from the damp hollow to Schwarz's left.

Schwarz shook his head. "Ghosts, man. That's all I see—ghosts."

Davis appeared, his jacket shiny with blood, his eyes inflamed with either grief or rage. "Danny's had it," he whispered. "Didn't even know what hit him."

"Where's Renny?" Lyons asked.

"Right here," Lussac replied from a particularly foul hole of weeds below a fallen log.

"Then talk to me," Lyons said. "Tell me what kind of game they're playing."

"Like I said," Lussac replied softly, "they believe themselves to be serving Eshu, Lord of the Closed Paths. Most likely they're fighting according to a plan derived from the Eshu Skull, which is the Black God's number one assistant."

"So how would you suggest we hit back?"

"Way I figure it," Lussac said softly, "we've got two choices at this point. We could call in the state troopers, maybe even the National Guard. That kind of firepower will make mincemeat of even Eshu's followers."

"And the second choice?" Lyons asked, thinking about Carrie Latrobe, knowing they didn't have much time.

"The second choice," Lussac replied, "is to show them they're backing a false god. Show them they can go ahead and call down the whole black circus of Eshu, but it still ain't going to stop our bullets."

"Renny's right, Carl," Schwarz whispered. "We've got to show them their magic isn't going to protect them anymore."

Lyons took another ten or twenty seconds to scan the terrain while continuing to think about Carrie. Then, finally turning to Blancanales, he asked, "How about it, Pol? Do you think we can show them their magic doesn't work?"

LOUIS LECLOUD PULLED OUT another magazine, inserted it into his weapon and slid a little deeper into the damp tangle of vines. Beside him Charlie Durange and the Florabel brothers also prepared themselves to repel a second assault on the stronghold of Eshu the Bold. Closer to the house, ten to twenty more believers fingered their weapons in anticipation of the unbelievers' attack. Although they were all nervous, none of them had forgotten what Baby had said: battles weren't won by shooting flesh and blood with bullets; they were won by casting spells in the sky.

"You're not fighting for me," Baby had told them. "You're fighting for the gods who dwell above us. You're fighting for your fathers and your fathers before them." He had also told them that they were fighting for Africa and the memory of those who couldn't fight.

Crows cawed somewhere over the swamp, creatures Baby had always counted as personal friends. And crickets, also friends of Baby, throbbed steadily in the willows. All of nature worked on the side of Baby Shu Duval, especially the children of the night.

LeCloud's last thought concerned an owl or raven that flapped just above him in an oak tree. Even after the bullet pierced his forehead, splitting his brain in half, he still continued to believe that the gods were watching over him.

BLANCANALES HELD HIS BREATH, consciously telling himself, *You are nothing. You are part of the tree, the leaves, the moss, the branches. Nothing.*

In all he had spent fifteen minutes positioning himself in the cypress. Because he needed the height, he'd chosen one of the upper branches, some thirty feet above the marshy ground. He had then spent another six minutes cloaking himself in a sheet of moss, and another two minutes scanning the trembling willows through the night vision system. But when he finally found his target, aiming three inches above the right eye, he lapsed into a familiar zone of timelessness, not thinking, not breathing, not even consciously squeezing the trigger, but rather just letting it happen.

He squeezed off a second round as another silhouette appeared above the willows, and saw the bulky form shudder with the impact before crashing into the leaves. Then, noting a movement in the grass near the water, he squeezed off two more shots.

In response a long burst of AK-47 autofire erupted from the swamp grass. But by now Blancanales was firmly under the spell of his own kind of magic—the magic of a silent sniper.

He pressed himself against the mossy trunk as five or six slugs cut through the branches around him. Then, lowering his eye to the sight and pulling the butt into his shoulder, he squeezed off yet another shot and heard choked cries from the clump of tiger lilies, catching a brief glimpse of someone thrashing in the willows.

Then Politician locked onto three more ghostly figures in the grass, three more wide-eyed believers who would soon come to realize that even Eshu couldn't protect them from a high-powered sniper rifle.

"LET'S GO," Lyons whispered. "Let's move out."

He rose from the foliage like a stalking beast, his Heckler & Koch in the crook of his arm, his eyes fixed on the willows beyond the marsh. Behind him came Lussac and Davis, while Schwarz fanned out to the right. When they passed the first line of trees, at least four targets presented themselves.

Lyons didn't open up, though, until he glimpsed someone emerging from the vines. He fired two long bursts, spraying hot lead in a wide arc, then concentrating on the screams. The targets were catapulted into the air, shuddering in a spray of blood before finally collapsing into a heap of shattered limbs.

There were screams farther away now, and someone shouted, "Kill them!" But when they sighted two more men scrambling out of the reeds, Lyons and Schwarz leveled their weapons and squeezed off fifteen rounds between them.

The first killer grunted under the impact, then skidded into the tall grass as bits of skull spun off his head in crazy circles. But the second man only trembled a little, as if shrugging off the four shells that had hit his chest.

"He's wearing a vest!" Schwarz shouted as he watched the second man turn with a crazed scream and point his AK at Lyons.

But even before Ironman could make sense of the warning, there were seven clean blasts from Lussac's Remington shotgun, which blew Baby Duval's zombie to perdition.

Then there was silence, thick, absolute silence that seemed to paralyze the woods.

"Maybe we should call in the backup," Lussac suggested. "Hell, maybe we should call in the Marines."

Lyons shook his head. "There isn't time. If we're going to get Carrie out of there alive, we've got to move in right now."

They reached the high willows and the last rank of mossy oaks that lined the unpaved road. Although the mist lay thick among the tangled vines and ivy, there was still a fairly clear view of the house.

"So how do you want to play it?" Schwarz asked.

Lyons looked at Lussac, then at Davis. Finally he took a deep breath. "I guess I want you guys to cover me while I go inside and get Carrie."

"You make it sound pretty simple," Davis said.

"It is," Lyons breathed. "It's real simple."

But even before he rose from the grass, the air filled with the complex rhythms of conga drums and chanting voices.

"They're calling down the spirits," Lussac said. "For a last stand."

## 16

Duval moved his torso from the waist, swaying like a hypnotized elephant to the rhythm of the drums. His glazed eyes were fixed on the flickering candles, his left hand still on the unconscious woman's breast.

"Snap out of it!" Dawson ordered. "You hear me? Snap out of it!"

Duval just smiled, though, and whispered, *"Gris-gris. Gris-gris. Quimbanda."*

Dawson moved to one end of the basement, loosened his collar and collapsed on a sofa. "I think you fail to grasp the seriousness of this situation," he told Duval. "They're about to storm this house and kill us!"

Once again Duval just smiled. "You feel it, too, don't you?" he asked. "Even though you don't believe, you still feel it in your bones, your blood, the very core of your soul. Eshu the Sly Dealer is with us!"

A stringy Creole appeared in the basement doorway, a coppery killer called Jesus Fever. "They be coming in soon," he said.

Dawson turned to Duval. "You hear that? They're about to kick down the goddamn door!"

But Baby just grinned. "Then kill them," he whispered, giggling. "Kill them and catch their souls in a jar."

Dawson shifted his gaze back to the Creole, then up at the ceiling where, two floors above, another crazed believer pounded on a conga drum. It was hopeless, he thought. Having created the myth, he couldn't break the spell.

He rose from the sofa, moved to a grimy wooden table and picked up a bottle of white powder. "See this?" he said, holding the bottle in front of Duval's grinning face. "Do you see this? This is your *gris-gris*. A chemical derived from a fish. You inject it into the blood and it causes temporary paralysis. There's no magic or spirits. It's just chemistry!"

From the wooden table he moved to the far wall and picked up a voice-activated microphone. "And what about this?" he yelled. "This is your pipeline to the spirits—a sixty-five-dollar transmitter!" Then, sweeping his arm across the shelves and sending all sorts of plastic body parts flying, he bellowed, "It's a hoax! It's just a goddamn hoax!"

Duval stopped swaying and looked at Dawson. "You have no right. I am Baby Shu. I am the son of Eshu, and you have no right to speak to me this way."

"I have no right, eh? Well, let me tell you something, Baby. I don't just advise you. I created you. Do you understand what I'm saying? I created you!"

Then, although something genuinely terrible seemed to pass across Duval's face, he finally stopped grinning. "Okay, maybe we play it your way for a little while longer."

The echo of drums ceased and was replaced by the crack of sporadic gunfire. There were also cries from the parlor and a chorus of harsh whispers from the stairwell. Despite the pandemonium above, however, the basement couldn't have been quieter. Duval sat on the floor, his eyes glued to a flickering candle. Jesus Fever stood guard at the doorway, an AK-47 in his arms.

"We have to buy a little time," Dawson said. "That's the first thing. We have to buy time until my team from Langley arrives."

Duval nodded, but still kept staring at the candle. "And when do these white boys of yours arrive?"

"Soon," Dawson replied, ignoring Duval's insulting tone. "Very soon."

Another of Duval's followers suddenly appeared in the doorway and whispered something in Jesus Fever's ear. The Creole then turned to Dawson. "Jackie say dey close."

Dawson took a moment to digest Fever's words, then glanced at Carrie's body on the floor. "Well, obviously it's the girl they want."

Duval placed his hand on Carrie's forehead and ran a finger along the curve of her lips. "They may want her," he mumbled. "But they ain't going to get her. They ain't going to get her because she's mine. Mine!"

Dawson shook his head with another frustrated sigh, then crossed the room and sank into a chair near Duval. "Now listen to me very carefully. Those men out there don't give a shit about your so-called *quimbunda*. They don't care about your damn *gris-gris* and your damn spirits. All they care about is that girl, which means she can be our ticket out of here. Now if you want to try to meet them head-on with your mumbo jumbo, that's your business, but I'm going to use her as a bargaining chip. Is that clear?"

Duval frowned. "What do you mean, bargaining chip?"

Dawson reached down and took hold of Carrie's wrist. Her pulse was weak but steady. "I intend to trade her for our freedom. Now I can either cut you in on that deal, or I can leave you here to die. It's your choice."

Duval removed Dawson's hand from Carrie's wrist, then pressed a finger against Dawson's chest. "She ain't no bargaining chip. She's mine. Her body, her soul—mine and mine alone."

Dawson stared at the ceiling, then looked at Jesus Fever. "Look, we don't have time to argue about this. They'll be coming in here any minute. We've got to get her upstairs and start the negotiations."

"No way," Duval grunted, getting to his feet. "There's no way you're going to trade my woman for anything, not when I still have power to fight them."

"Power?" Dawson smirked and got to his feet. "Your power? I'm your power! Me!"

But even as he spoke these words, he caught a glimpse of something in Baby's eyes he'd never seen before, something dark and cold, limitless and furious. Twenty seconds passed, a full minute, and still Duval kept looking at him, staring at him, reaching out with a cold hand.

"You know what, Mr. Charlie?" he finally whispered. "I think maybe I don't need you anymore."

"What are you talking about, you stupid idiot? You're nothing without me. Nothing but another Haitian beggar."

Duval turned and motioned to Jesus Fever. The Creole fired from the hip, hardly even bothering to look. The first burst lifted Dawson into the air and tossed him against the wall. The second burst pounded his chest into pulp.

"And now your soul is also mine," Baby Duval whispered. "And your power." He stared at Dawson's body for a while, swaying to some personal rhythm of his own, his lips spreading in an enigmatic smile.

"Go tell the others," he finally said to Fever. "Go tell the others that my power will make them win."

The Creole hesitated for a moment, as if there were something in Baby's eyes that he, too, had never seen before, something he desperately needed to nourish him, to sustain him, to make him strong. Then, finally, he moved out into the unlighted corridor.

Alone again, Duval turned his attention to Carrie and knelt beside her. He stroked her forehead, arms, hips and belly, then brushed his lips against her ear, whispering, "Come, my dear, it's time to descend. It's time to join Eshu." Gathering her up in his arms, he moved out into the corridor, where he could hear gunfire. At the moment, though, all he was aware of was the faintly beating heart of Carrie Latrobe. "Yes, your soul belongs to me now," he whispered into her ear. "Me alone."

LYONS PAUSED just inside the doorway. Among the shards of broken glass and fragments of splintered oak in the foyer lay the bodies of two men who had fallen under the hail of covering fire. The first, a muscular Haitian, had taken two slugs in the base of the spine and a third in the back of the head. His left hand still clutched some sort of amulet. The second, obviously hit while attempting to reach one of the upstairs bedrooms, was sprawled on the staircase. Struck in the stomach, he had probably taken a long time to die...time enough to scrawl an inverted cross in blood on the plaster.

There were sounds of footsteps behind him, then the gentle click of a safety being released. Lyons whirled, ready to fire, but saw that it was only Lussac.

Lyons smiled. "Didn't I tell you to stay back?"

"Not exactly," Lussac replied. "Besides, it's still my case."

From the doorway they moved in a half crouch into the shadowy foyer. Here, too, there were various signs in blood on the walls: pitchforks within circles, inverted triangles and what looked like the face of a devil.

"It's part of the consecration process," Lussac whispered. "You see, Eshu has many forms and assistants and each one has a different sign."

Lyons pointed to a butchered rooster dangling from the kitchen doorway. "What's that?"

Lussac grimaced. "That marks the boundary between heaven and hell."

They could hear drumbeats on the second floor and chanting. Then, along the corridor to the master bedroom, the first leering figure emerged from the shadows. He sported a pair of four-inch plastic fangs.

"Maybe you should try to talk to him," Lyons suggested. "Tell him he's under arrest."

Lussac leveled his shotgun and took a step back. "You're kidding, aren't you?"

The black killer slowly drew a rusty butcher's knife from the folds of his filthy raincoat. Then, broadening his fanged grin, he started forward, advancing with stiff, unsteady steps, the knife trembling slightly in his hand.

"Is he drugged?" Lyons asked as he backed against the wall.

"Not exactly," Lussac replied.

"Then what?"

"He's under Baby's control."

Lyons aimed his SMG at the zombie's chest. The killer paused, then charged. Lyons squeezed off six rounds, and the attacker shuddered, but continued forward. Lussac fired three quick blasts and knocked the zombie against the wall. But still he stayed on his feet. Finally Lyons blew the man's head away.

"Don't ask me," Lussac muttered. "I don't know any more than you, so don't even ask."

There were echoes of more drums at the end of the corridor, but no signs of life beyond a half-gutted chicken still quivering on the floor. Voices reverberated throughout the house and in the walls. But as they advanced they encountered no more zombies.

Just then Schwarz and Blancanales appeared, followed by Massard, Davis and three more cops from the backup team. After a cursory search of the ground floor, Lyons assembled them in the parlor. Although the voices and drums had stopped, they could now smell burnt rubber and sulfur.

"Maybe they split," Davis suggested. "Maybe they left by the back door and headed out to the swamp."

Ignoring the comment, Lyons moved to Lussac's side and drew him away from the others. "Where do you think they hold their rituals?"

Lussac glanced around the parlor, first fixing his gaze on the doorway to the pantry. "Yeah, you're right. They're in their temple."

"Which would be where?" Blancanales asked.

Lussac glanced at a second door, half opened on a dark flight of wooden steps. "The basement. Down there."

They moved in single file, Lyons on point again, followed by Schwarz and Lussac. There were more crude pitchforks and circles on the wall—some in chalk, some in blood. Beyond the steps stretched a dark basement passage littered with rat droppings.

There were also pools of water and the stench of rotting flesh.

"All these old places were built with secret passages," Lussac whispered. "Some of them extend for miles."

"Would there be another way out to the surface?" Lyons asked.

Lussac nodded. "Probably, but I don't think Duval's looking to escape. I think he intends to meet us down here where he thinks his powers are strongest."

There were shifting shadows at the end of the corridor. But it wasn't until Lyons reached the first turn that he finally caught a glimpse of something tangible, something inching toward him along the edge of the passage, steadily, silently, intently.

He pressed himself against the brick and squeezed off a dozen frantic rounds at the snake. Then he fired again at what looked like a second snake and saw the slender body explode.

When Schwarz shone his flashlight ahead of them, however, all they found were bits of rubber and splattered plastic. "Don't let it bother you, Carl. It could easily have been real."

There were more shifting shadows where the passage dropped to a vaulted gallery, then definite echoes of footsteps in shallow water. But this time Lyons saw nothing until the bullets started flying.

"Down!" he shouted as the first burst of AK-47 and M-16 fire slammed into the bricks around him. "Get down!"

Another burst lanced out of the darkness ahead, and there were muffled cries from a narcotics officer named Salinger. Then, following what sounded like the bark of a Colt .45, Davis fell back with a fist-sized hole in his chest.

"Leave him!" Lyons shouted to Lussac. "He's finished." Then, after unleashing a blind spray from his MP-5, Ironman scrambled back with the others to where the passage descended to even deeper pools of water.

They waited in foul water up to their knees. A deeper stench of decay filled their nostrils while unseen rats moved along a ledge above.

"This is great," Massard said in the inky blackness. "This is really fucking great. Pinned down in a cesspool by a bunch of goddamn zombies."

"Take it easy, Oz," Lussac soothed. He peered at Lyons. "So what do we do now?"

"We give 'em a little of our own voodoo," Lyons replied. He turned to Blancanales and held up an open hand. Blancanales nodded without smiling, then pulled out a stainless-steel canister.

"What the hell?" Massard whispered.

"Flash grenade," Schwarz said.

Next came the clips—one in Lyons's hand, three more for his pockets. Then, following an elaborate exchange of hand signals, Lyons led Schwarz and Blancanales back down the passage.

For the first fifty feet or so Lyons fixed his attention on practical matters. He wriggled forward on his belly, his face in and out of the stinking water, while rats scurried around him. But his main concern was that Dawson might have equipped his people with night vision systems that would allow them to penetrate the pitch-black. But he wasn't concerned about the *gris-gris*, the *quimbanda*, the walking dead or any other mumbo jumbo. He was past all that.

There were faint echoes of more voices ahead, and what might have been a woman's scream. And there were more drumbeats as well as a peal of muffled laughter. Duval and Carrie were up ahead. He was certain.

Lyons brought his men to a halt. He could see Duval's people now—six, maybe seven dim figures waiting in the darker shadows. Lyons held up three fingers. Blancanales nodded and passed the gesture along to Schwarz.

A harsh voice called out an unintelligible name. Although the drums were still faint, the rhythm grew increasingly frantic. Then, counting off another thirty seconds, Lyons slowly rose to a crouch and pulled out the flash grenade.

He tossed it almost gently, turning his face away and shutting his eyes. A moment before the blinding flash and deafening crack, he clamped his hands to his ears. There were cries, but he hardly heard them. There were shots, but he ignored them entirely. Someone might have shouted another name, but it was lost in his own outraged scream.

He fired from a half crouch at the disoriented figures ahead. Behind him and to his left, Schwarz and

Blancanales also unleashed a hail of lead into the jerking shadows, knocking at least five of them down.

"Let's go!" Lyons shouted. "Go! Go! Go!"

There were more screams as Lyons advanced and sprayed another burst of lead into the crumbling figures. He caught a glimpse of something spinning off into the blackness, then heard an agonized moan as a bloody torso suddenly materialized in front of him. He squeezed another six rounds into a terrified face and watched a heavy black man fall like a brick wall. Then, turning at the sound of another desperate moan, he found himself gazing into a face only inches away from his own.

It was a face he might have seen before, an oddly boyish face with wide eyes and a thin growth above the lip. Although disfigured with theatrical makeup, the face was intensely alive, intensely human. And for a moment, an awful second or two, that sense of humanity froze Lyons, actually kept him from squeezing the trigger. Then, screaming with all his might, he emptied the rest of the clip. The face shattered into a thousand pieces before the body fell.

Lyons pressed himself against the wall between Schwarz and Blancanales. Although Politician held a flashlight, Lyons wouldn't let him switch it on. Not yet. Not with the hint of something still approaching from deep within the vaulted gallery.

There were sounds of footsteps, a soft, strangely slow tread drawing closer and closer. There were also strains of someone singing a toneless, childish melody.

Then, by degrees, there was even a faint outline, a shy ghost materializing out of the shadows.

"What do you make of it?" Blancanales whispered.

Lyons shook his head. "I don't know."

"Well, how about we shoot first and ask questions later?" Schwarz asked as he jammed another magazine into his SMG.

But before he could level the weapon, Lyons clamped a hand on the barrel. "Hold on! It's Carrie."

She seemed to emerge in pieces, first as a floating white dress, then as a strangely pale face, finally as two extended hands clutching fragmentation grenades.

"Carl," Blancanales whispered. "Carl!"

"I see them," Lyons whispered back.

"So what the hell is she doing?" Schwarz asked.

But Lyons just shook his head and continued to watch her advance.

She moved with slow steps, her eyes blank, her arms at stiff angles to her body. Although the water must have been cold on her bare feet, she didn't seem conscious of it. She didn't seem conscious of anything.

"He's hypnotized her," Schwarz whispered.

"Or drugged her," Lyons said.

"Well, either way we'd better do something fast," Blancanales said. "Because those grenades are live."

The girl seemed to hesitate when Lyons rose from the shadows to meet her gaze. But although she continued to look at him, to meet his gaze fully, her own eyes remained dead.

"Carrie," Lyons called out. There was no response, not even another hesitation.

"Carrie. It's me, Lyons."

Still nothing. And Blancanales was right—the grenades were live, kept from exploding only by the pressure of her hands against the firing mechanism.

"Carrie, listen to me."

But she just continued walking toward them, her eyes lifeless in the glare of Politician's flashlight.

"Carrie, listen to me. It's Lyons. Carl Lyons."

"It's not going to work," Schwarz said. "She doesn't even hear you."

"Carrie," Lyons whispered again.

Schwarz released the safety on his weapon and shifted his finger to the trigger. "Got no choice," he breathed. "She's not going to stop."

"Carrie, for God's sake, it's me, Lyons!"

Then, although her eyes still registered nothing, she mumbled, "Carl...Carl..." There were also large tears rolling down her cheeks now. "Carl..."

He came to her slowly and whispered, "Don't let go, baby. Don't release your grip." Then, placing his hands over hers, he gently removed the grenades and passed them back to Schwarz. By the time he drew her back into the shadows, she was crying softly but freely, her face buried in his chest. Lyons held her very tightly and whispered, "Where's Duval?"

At first she just shook her head and pressed her face even harder against his chest. Then, very softly, she whispered, "Everywhere. He's everywhere."

And, judging by the peals of laughter that suddenly rolled out from the walls around them, it seemed to be true—the bastard was everywhere.

**17**

There were two flights of stone steps below the point where they had found Carrie. The steps were ancient, cut from solid rock and descending into an equally solid darkness. In the moments before moving down the steps, Lyons told himself he had to maintain a logical perspective. But in the end there was only the damp blackness, the echo of dripping water and a softer echo of voices.

Lussac appeared again, and behind him stood Massard and four other cops. Following a whispered exchange at the top of the steps, it was decided that only Lussac would join Able Team for the final descent into Baby's lair.

The descent began with a long, slow crawl through more brackish water. Shining a flashlight on the wall, they saw drawings of pitchforks within circles, pentagrams, triangles and grim devil faces.

"What's it supposed to signify?" Lyons asked, examining a particularly gruesome portrait of a devil.

"It means this is unholy ground," Lussac replied. "It means we're approaching the physical seat of Baby's power."

At the bottom of the first flight of steps they found chicken and pig bones.

"Eshu's repast," Lussac whispered. "He can generally be enticed out of the sky with whiskey and cigars, but sometimes it takes a little more to keep him satisfied."

Farther along the passage where the walls were wet with seepage, Lyons found himself staring at a human hand nailed to the bricks. Then came the other hand, a foot and finally the toes.

"Looks like ol' Eshu's really having himself a party tonight," Lussac whispered. "Looks like he's really getting himself worked up into a frenzy."

"Yeah, but who's the victim?" Lyons asked.

"Could be anyone," Schwarz said, stooping to examine the hand. "Could have even been one of us."

There were traces of intestines smeared along the lower walls and bits of bloody clothing hanging from the vaulted ceiling. But it wasn't until they reached the mouth of the main chamber that they finally saw the head—Charlie Dawson's head, gazing in blank horror from an iron spike embedded in the wall.

"Mr. Charlie always did say he'd keep an eye on me," a voice roared from the darkness.

Lyons flattened himself against the bricks and peered into the torch-lighted chamber. Although he couldn't actually see Duval, he knew, somehow, that the voice belonged to his quarry. Lussac and Blancanales drew their weapons while Schwarz pulled out a grenade.

For the moment, however, there were still no targets except for flickering shadows.

"How about I try to talk to him?" Lussac whispered. "See if we can locate him that way?"

Lyons shrugged. "Sure, go ahead."

There was a narrow recess below the arched entrance to the chamber. Sliding past Lyons and into the recess, Lussac shouted, "Baby!"

He was greeted by silence, broken only by the sound of conga drums and dripping water.

"Baby, do you know who this is?"

More silence, this time broken only by what sounded like a footstep.

"Baby, do you hear me? I'm talking to you!"

A hollow chuckle was followed by what might have been the rattle of bones.

"Baby, you goddamn son of bitch, I'm talking to you!"

Then, very softly, Duval whispered, "But, of course, you're talking to me."

"Baby, give it up. It's over."

In response Duval only laughed again, and now Lussac could see shadows drawing closer.

"Duval, I'm telling you to give up."

"And I," Duval snarled from somewhere very close, possibly no more than eight or ten feet beyond the arch, "am telling you to die!"

Lussac waited a few more seconds before reacting to the approaching shadows. Then, springing out from the wall and sliding like a skater across the mossy bricks, he faced them with his Remington shotgun.

There were three figures just beyond the arch, three ghostly zombies with automatic rifles and kitchen knives in their belts. But given the speed and fury of Lussac's attack, they didn't have a chance.

Lussac shot at their heads, figuring they were probably clad in bulletproof vests. Dropping to his knees below a rain of autofire, he pumped four more shells into the killers' bellies. And, as Able Team's weapons joined the firefight, the noise of gunfire became deafening.

But still Duval's men kept coming, moving like robots out of the blackness, their knees barely bending, their eyes locked on nothing, faces entirely expressionless. Although some carried automatic weapons, others were armed only with knives, bottles and iron pipes.

"This is insane!" Lussac yelled. "This is completely insane! Die, damn you!"

Five or six more figures appeared on his left, half-dead eyes staring straight ahead, legs stiffly carrying them forward.

And as still more zombies appeared, moving stiffly into the torchlight, Lussac had no choice but to open up with his shotgun again. He fired six more shells, pounding his targets into mincemeat.

And still they kept on coming, dead-eyed, stiff-limbed and silent.

Insane.

When it was finally over, Lussac slumped against the slime-encrusted bricks and shut his eyes. Beside him Schwarz and Blancanales also took a moment to catch their breath, while Lyons just stared at the carnage around him. In all he counted fifteen bodies among the pools of blood and stagnant water, fifteen victims of suicide. Some still wore their grotesque masks. Most still clutched amulets. All were really dead now.

"Why?" Blancanales asked softly. "Why?"

Lussac shook his head. "I guess that's something we'll have to ask Duval."

FOR A LONG TIME after the shooting stopped Duval remained seated in the darkness. He sat in a high-backed chair emblazoned with heads of serpents and jaguars. He sat with a massive cigar between his thumb and index finger and a necklace of cowrie shells dangling from his wrists. Squatting on the floor beside him were Jesus Fever and a Haitian named Etienne Monroe. Behind Duval's chair, also squatting on the damp floor, were five more believers. Most were shirtless and barefoot. None held rifles.

Duval's remaining followers chanted and rocked back and forth. Their eyes, even after Lyons and his team appeared, remained fixed on the torches along the far wall, while Baby's eyes remained on the pyramid of clay jars that supposedly held the souls of his flock.

The stout black man finally turned his attention to the arched entrance of his chamber when Lyons and the others appeared. He didn't shift his body, didn't speak, didn't even open his mouth. All that moved were his eyes. Then, by degrees, like slow-melting wax, his lips spread into a thin smile. "Welcome. Welcome to the throne of Eshu."

Lyons met the man's gaze, but only for a moment. Then, letting his eyes gradually scan the room, he stared at the pyramid of clay jars heaped against the far wall. In the flickering torchlight it almost looked as if the jars were moving, gently rocking back and forth as the souls inside them tried to escape.

"My children," Duval said softly. "The immortal souls of all my children."

Lyons heard the scrape of a footstep from one of the darker alcoves behind Duval's chair, but he ignored it. When Duval finally withdrew something from the folds of his white silk robe, however, Lyons leveled his SMG.

"Miss Latrobe," Duval smiled, holding up another clay jar. "The beautiful soul of Miss Carrie Latrobe is safely imprisoned in this pot." He put the jar aside and withdrew a second jar, this one sealed with wax and decorated with tiny pentagrams. "And this is our famous Mr. Dawson, should you be wondering what became of him."

"How about you let me waste the bastard?" Blancanales whispered.

Before Lyons could respond, though, Lussac joined them at the top of the stairs. "This is still my case, Carl."

"Yeah," Lyons rasped, lowering his weapon and stepping aside. "It's still your case."

Lussac remained in the shadows for a moment or two, then cocked his shotgun and stepped out to confront Duval.

The Haitian smiled. "Ah, Monsieur Renny Lussac, my great friend. How good to finally see you."

Lussac raised his shotgun, pointing the muzzle at Duval's ample belly. "It's over, Baby. All over."

Duval shifted his gaze slightly to the left, possibly glancing at the pyramid of jars, possibly at something else that lay behind the halo of torchlight. "Over?" He grinned, his gold teeth glinting like tiny flashbulbs. "Over? But how can you say it's over when it's just beginning?"

Lussac shook his head and raised the Remington, keeping an eye on Fever and Monroe, both of whom seemed harmless now.

"He's right, Inspector," a fair-haired man said from the darkness suddenly. "It's only just beginning."

The lean man stepped out of the shadows with a casual swagger. Although not visibly armed, Lyons was pretty certain he was packing something underneath his checked sport coat. Behind him stood two more pale figures: a balding but muscular man with a Smith & Wesson .357 and a paunchy Hispanic with an Uzi.

Lyons knew immediately that they were CIA. He could spot one a mile away. Looking more closely at the lean, fair-haired man, Lyons finally recognized him. Hal Brognola, the chief of Stony Man operations, had a file on the guy a foot thick. He was a nasty piece of business. Ugly Americans didn't come any uglier. "James Potter," he finally said out loud.

"My reputation precedes me," the lean man said, smiling dangerously. "But you have me at a disadvantage. I don't think I know you, though you're damn good to get this far."

"What do you want?" Lyons asked, not bothering to disguise his disgust.

Potter shrugged and brushed a lock of blond hair from his eyes. "What do you think we want?"

Schwarz and Blancanales stepped out from behind Lyons, their weapons pointed at the CIA men. Lussac still covered Baby Duval.

Potter grinned. "Justice, right? You guys are from Justice."

Ignoring the question, Politician shifted his SMG until the muzzle was pointed at Potter's face. "This is a closed party, pal. Why don't you and your two goons take a hike?"

Potter stuffed his hands into the pockets of his white trousers. "Well, the fact is, boys, we happen to have an invitation from the host."

"He also got himself an invitation from Eshu of the Void," Duval crowed. "And let me tell you, that definitely counts for something big."

Lyons ignored the crazy Haitian and stared hard at Potter, his eyes now reduced to slits, his finger on the trigger of his SMG. "Ride on, Potter," he said softly. "Pack up your men and head back to Langley."

Potter smiled again and glanced at his patent leather shoes. "Look, how about we talk privately? What do you say, a little private chat, just you, me and the inspector here?''

Lyons glanced at Lussac, and the Cajun nodded. ''All right, we'll talk.''

They withdrew to an alcove at the far end of the chamber. Although Lyons's view of Duval was somewhat limited from the alcove, it was obvious the man was growing bored. He sipped whiskey from a hip flask and toyed with another clay jar.

''Okay, so the guy's a bastard,'' Potter began, peering past Lyons at the outline of Duval slouched in his shabby throne. ''So the guy's a complete mental case and a killer to boot. But the fact is, we need him. We need him bad.''

''And when you say, 'we,''' Lussac said, ''you mean?''

''He means the Agency,'' Lyons muttered.

Potter flashed a quick smile. ''Look, I'm not trying to kid you. We want Duval. We want his influence in Haiti and we want the secrets of the tetrodotoxin shit.''

''The man's a murderer,'' Lussac countered. ''And that makes him mine.''

''And how many more murders are you going to have on your books if the wrong people get their hands on that voodoo powder? You saw what that shit can do. What if somebody were to use it to create an army? What if the other guys got hold of it? You know, the Commies. We're on the same side, after all, aren't we?''

Lussac looked at Lyons, then shifted his eyes back to the outline of Duval and shook his head. "Sounds like you got it all figured out."

Potter shrugged. "It's a tactical decision, that's all. I don't believe in this voodoo crap any more than you do, but the fact remains that a lot of people *do* believe, people the Agency needs to stem the flow of communism in the Southern Hemisphere. Now obviously Duval's a psycho, but in the right circumstances, with the right kind of handler, he might just prove to be a very valuable psycho."

"And what happens when Duval starts murdering innocent people again?" Lussac asked. "What happens when he gets it in his head that Eshu wants another human sacrifice?"

Potter shrugged. "Hey, nobody said there wasn't a risk factor. When you're trying to stop the expansion of communism, there's always going to be a risk factor."

Lussac glanced at Lyons again, but the blond commando said nothing, so Lussac just shook his head. "I'm sorry, but it's no deal. Duval's my suspect. He's wanted in connection with the murder of a New Orleans police officer and at least four others. He's going to stand trial. If he's proven innocent, you can have him then, but not before."

Potter shifted his eyes to his associate from Langley. "Well, then, I guess we've got a problem. I guess we've got one hell of a problem, because one way or another I'm taking Duval."

At that moment Lyons glimpsed someone moving out of the shadows, a thin figure in a white gown. "I don't think anyone's going to be taking Duval anywhere except maybe in a body bag."

Carrie moved purposely across the chamber floor until she came within ten feet of Duval. Although Schwarz and the others had called out her name, begging her to stop, they didn't dare approach, not with the Colt Python in her hands leveled at Baby Duval's head.

"Do something!" Duval shouted. "Somebody do something!"

But when Potter's men attempted to raise their weapons, Schwarz and Blancanales responded in kind, leveling their SMGs in defense of the girl and shaking their heads. "You guys even breathe too hard and you're dead," Blancanales said.

"Tell her to put it down," Potter pleaded with Lyons.

"I don't think so, Potter. I think it's her call."

For a long time Carrie couldn't seem to make up her mind. She remained almost motionless, the Python extending from her outstretched arms, her unblinking eyes fixed on Baby's forehead.

"Will somebody please do something!" Duval shouted, his face bathed in perspiration. Then, turning to meet Carrie's gaze, he held up the clay jar. "Hey, you want back your soul? Okay, I give it back. Go on, take it!"

"Goddamn it, Lussac, do something!" Potter yelled.

And Baby also shouted, "Do something! Somebody please do some—"

Finally Carrie squeezed the trigger. She fired with her eyes wide open and her lips slightly parted. She fired with her whole hand, riding out the kick of the big gun and then firing again. The first slug entered Duval's left eye and ripped out the back of his skull. The second shot entered his chest and punched through his ribs.

For a moment, after the gunfire, it almost seemed as if Duval were unhurt. Then, like a taut bow, he slowly slid from his throne. As he fell, the clay jar containing Carrie's soul slipped from his fingers and shattered on the bricks. But Carrie didn't seem to mind. She was smiling at Lyons, her eyes alive once more.

# Epilogue

Nothing, Lussac thought, is coincidental in New Orleans.

It was half past six in the morning. After waiting until the coroner arrived and the last of the zombies were hauled off, Lussac and Able Team returned to the city. They crossed the causeway on the heels of another storm, sticking close to the river's edge. As the sun rose, the fog suddenly lifted and the rain stopped...at last. All the time Able Team had been in New Orleans, fog and rain had dogged them.

Lussac flipped another cigarette between his lips and grinned. "Ain't nothing coincidental in New Orleans."

"So what happens now?" Blancanales asked as they sped along.

Lussac shrugged. "A little talk. A little flurry of papers. Maybe a funeral or two."

"And what are we going to do about Potter?" Blancanales asked.

"Oh, I don't know," Lussac said. "But somehow I get the feeling the CIA has had just about enough of this city for a while."

"And Carrie?" Lyons asked.

Lussac frowned. "Who's Carrie?"

They drove along the waterfront past loading docks and the crumbling arcade. A sleepy boy in a ragged tuxedo tap-danced on a stretch of littered pavement, while a girl in a tattered dress swept the terrace of a basement café.

"Like I was saying the other day," Lussac said, "New Orleans isn't just a city. It's a frame of mind. Take what happened last night, for instance. Now that ol' Mr. James Potter, he's probably going to say Miss Carrie had something to do with Baby getting shot and all. Why, he might even suggest we press charges against Miss Carrie Latrobe, least of all for shooting Baby Duval."

"So who does get charged with Duval's murder?" Schwarz asked.

Lussac shrugged. "Hell, I don't know. With all those bullets flying around last night, it could have been anyone, right?"

"And what happens when the Agency decides that maybe Charlie Dawson wasn't so crazy after all?" Blancanales asked.

Lussac cocked his head and flicked his cigarette out the car window. "What do you mean?"

"He means that sooner or later someone in Langley could very well decide to try it all over again," Lyons said. "He means that you might not have heard the last of the Agency's psych-ops team."

Lussac stared out at the passing street. Beyond a line of moss-draped oaks lay another row of shuttered windows where murder was a possibility every day. "Don't worry. I'll be ready."

# DEATHLANDS.

## A different world—a different war

**RED EQUINOX**      $3.95  ☐
Ryan Cawdor and his band of postnuclear survivors enter a
malfunctioning gateway and are transported to Moscow, where
Americans are hated with an almost religious fervor and blamed
for the destruction of the world.

**DECTRA CHAIN**      $3.95  ☐
A gateway that is part of a rambling underwater complex brings
Ryan Cawdor and the group off the coast of what was once
Maine, where they are confronted with mutant creatures and
primitive inhabitants.

**ICE & FIRE**      $3.95  ☐
A startling discovery changes the lives of Ryan Cawdor and his
band of postholocaust survivors when they encounter several
cryogenically preserved bodies.

|  |  |
|---|---|
| Total Amount | $ _____ |
| Plus 75¢ Postage | _____.75 |
| Payment enclosed | $ _____ |

If you've missed any of these previous titles, please send a check or money order payable to Gold Eagle
Books.

| In the U.S. | In Canada |
|---|---|
| Gold Eagle Books | Gold Eagle Books |
| 901 Fuhrmann Blvd. | P.O. Box 609 |
| Box 1325 | Fort Erie, Ontario |
| Buffalo, NY 14269-1325 | L2A 5X3 |

**Please Print**

Name: _____

Address: _____

City: _____

State/Prov: _____

Zip/Postal Code: _____

DL-B1

More than action adventure...
books written by the men who were there

# VIETNAM: GROUND ZERO™
## ERIC HELM

Told through the eyes of an American Special Forces squad, an elite jungle fighting group of strike-and-hide specialists fight a dirty war half a world away from home.

These books cut close to the bone, telling it the way it really was.

"Vietnam at Ground Zero is where this book is written. The author has been there, and he knows. I salute him and I recommend this book to my friends."

—Don Pendleton
creator of *The Executioner*

"Helm writes in an evocative style that gives us Nam as it most likely was, without prettying up or undue bitterness."

—*Cedar Rapids Gazette*

"Eric Helm's Vietnam series embodies a literary standard of excellence. These books linger in the mind long after their reading."

—*Midwest Book Review*

Available wherever paperbacks are sold.

VIE 1

## by GAR WILSON

The battle-hardened five-man
commando unit known as Phoenix
Force continues its onslaught
against the hard realities of global
terrorism in an endless crusade for
freedom, justice and the rights of
the individual. Schooled in guerrilla
warfare, equipped with the latest in
lethal weapons, Phoenix Force's
adventures have made them a
legend in their own time. Phoenix
Force is the free world's foreign
legion!

"Gar Wilson is excellent! Raw action
attacks the reader on every page."
—Don Pendleton

Phoenix Force titles are available
wherever paperbacks are sold.

PF-1R

GOLD
EAGLE